MOTHERLAND

AND OTHER STORIES

WANDEKA GAYLE

MOTHERLAND

AND OTHER STORIES

PEEPAL TREE

First published in Great Britain in 2020
Peepal Tree Press Ltd
17 King's Avenue
Leeds LS6 1QS
England

ISBN13: 9781845234799

Supported using public funding by
ARTS COUNCIL
ENGLAND

ACKNOWLEDGEMENTS

It took a lot of support for me to create these stories about my beloved Caribbean people at home and abroad, drawn from memory, imagination and longing. The stories were written over several years and were first compiled in part as an element of my dissertation while I completed doctoral studies at the University of Lafayette in Louisiana in the Spring of 2018. I am eternally grateful for the guidance and support of acclaimed writer, John McNally, who chaired the committee and whom I still consider a mentor, and for the support of committee members Joanna Davis McElligatt, who inspired me to keep going when I often felt too different and isolated as a black Caribbean immigrant in a predominantly white institution, and Maria Seger for her infectious enthusiasm and encouragement through the process.

I would like to thank my family for their continued support, to my parents, Wezley Snr. and Sandra, for instilling a strong reading culture in their children from a very young age and for demonstrating the importance of stories; and to my siblings, Shawnette, Wezyann, Sanya and Wezley Jr. who have enriched my life and who inadvertently offered me material for stories through our very colourful conversations over the years.

To all my friends who became first readers of my work, especially Nikeisha Davis Jackson and Jason Knight, who continue to give me moral support.

To the black American, African and Caribbean fiction writers of Kimbilio Fiction and the Callaloo Creative Writer's Workshop who provided a safe haven, love, and vigorous critique of my work during our summer fellowships in the hills of New Mexico and the halls of Oxford University, where some of this work was conceived and produced.

Thank you to my second-form English teacher, Amos Thompson, who told me I would one day write a book, even before my thirteen-year-old mind could fully embrace that fact, and to all my writing professors who helped me to cultivate my love of words.

I must also acknowledge the literary journals and magazines where some of the stories found their first home:

My deepest appreciation to:

Transition Magazine, who published "The Blackout" in Fall 2020 in Issue 129; *Prairie Schooner*, who published "Walker Woman" in the Summer of 2020; *Blood Orange Review*, who published a version of "The Wish" in Spring 2020; *Kweli Journal*, for publishing "Prodigal" in Fall 2019, and for nominating it for the O. Henry Prize Stories 2020; *Pleiades*, for publishing a version of "Help Wanted" in Summer 2019, and for nominating it for a Pushcart Prize; *midnight & indigo*, for publishing "Finding Joy" in their inaugural issue in Winter 2018; *Interviewing The Caribbean*, for publishing "Cecile" in Winter 2018; *Moko, A Journal of Caribbean Art and Letters*, for publishing "Birdie" in November 2018; *Aaduna*, for publishing a version of "Reunion" (formerly "The Encounter") in Summer 2017; *Susumba*, for publishing "Melba" in Summer 2016. Thank you to Jeremy Poynting and team for giving them all a home.

Most of all, thank you to the divine muse, the ancestors, both literary and spiritual, and the preservers of the ancient, oral tradition whose folktales continue to inspire my work.

Thank you to all those who have said an encouraging word or found joy and meaning from my stories.

CONTENTS

Dedication

This is dedicated to all my black Caribbean women at
home and abroad,
whose stories the world often ignores.
I see you.

MOTHERLAND

Roxanne ran her hand over her tunic and looked down at her sturdy, white flats. She gazed out at the fog that hung like an omen over the street. She frowned at her reflection in the window. The damp made her short curls puffy and she had lost a few pounds, so her collarbone jutted out against the starkness of her uniform.

When she first arrived in London, she'd felt a surge of purpose and something akin to happiness. Maybe the towering old buildings, the tube and the double-decker red buses made her feel she'd moved on from Red Ground. She hadn't minded the perpetual cloudiness at first and the constant drinking of tea was comforting, even if there wasn't a sprig of fever grass or cerasee bush like her granny used to make.

"You have to have steel in you blood if you going over there," her father had said. "Is not like out here at all, at all."

"Don't frighten the child, Merlin," her granny had said.

"Well, some people think foreign is nice. Who feels it knows it."

He had gone to England in the fifties as a teenager, to what he still referred to as the motherland. He'd returned to Jamaica in the seventies, disillusioned. She had been born ten years after his return, when his resentment had crystallized into bitter rhetoric.

Would he be turning in his grave if he knew she had followed his footsteps? This was her life. Besides, he had hardly been around, leaving her with her grandparents after Roxanne's mother died. It was them she missed the most, but there was no going back; there was no one to go back to.

Six months before, she had looked down at her grandfather's face in the casket. How proper and polished he'd looked, hands crossed reverently across his chest. She had smiled to think how he would have laughed himself silly to see himself dressed in a crisp white shirt and a black, pin-striped suit.

Papa Jenkins had never worn a suit, even when he'd been forced to attend the Presbyterian church at the top of the hill – twice in the thirty-five years he had lived in Red Ground with the eternal red stain of the yam hills; there was no sense in washing it off when he was going back to dig some more the next day.

Papa's sister, Yvette, had offered to take her back with her to London after the funeral and Roxanne had agreed. This was before she discovered she was more housekeeper than house guest – ironing, washing, cooking, and cleaning. Finding a job and a flat of her own became an obsession; after three months, she was able to slip away.

Now, she was beginning to see beyond the museums and the quaint little cafes and long for the red dirt and her granny's cooking. She remembered that first morning at the care home when she popped her head in a room, looking for the office, and saw some staff members holding down an old man who vehemently refused to take his medicine. She learned later that he had refused to take it because the new nurse was Nigerian.

The Sunshine Nursing Home had near gothic stone walls and a general dreariness. Some days she looked down the gloomy corridors and expected to see shadowy figures flitting down them. It would be an awful place to come to die.

It was bad enough that she had to live above a middle-aged woman who stole the coins they needed to feed the electricity meter to buy her cigars, who insulted her at every turn.

"Do you practice voodoo or obeah in Jamaica?" Miss Carmen asked. "What about marijuana? I don't think our landlady would like that one bit."

The girls with whom she shared the upstairs rooms, American Fiona and Kenyan Asha, assured her she would get used to Miss Carmen but she never ceased to be amazed at the things that rolled out of the woman's mouth without seeming rancour.

"Dear me, those Asians can't speak to save their lives, but they do know how to make those darling little dumplings… Those Pakis are taking over our streets with their ram-shackle little shops… I love children about age two. Don't they look darling in their little jackets and mittens during winter, even the little dark ones?" And on and on…

"She better stop talking like that or one day, I go smack the dentures right out her head," Roxanne told Fiona.

Fiona laughed. "I just need to do one more semester and I'm getting the hell out of this house."

"You miss home too?" Roxanne asked.

Fiona smiled and turned grey eyes on her. They were stark in her brown face. She shrugged and slipped two giant hoops through her ear lobes.

"I mean. I shouldn't say it like that. It's not so bad with you here," she said. "Besides, why stress when you can go dancing? Right? You coming?"

Roxanne shook her head and began to peel off her uniform.

★

The next few weeks seemed to bleed into each other at Sunnyside. Two beds became vacant after their owners succumbed to a heart attack and kidney failure respectively. A new resident now occupied Room 38.

He was heavy set and sombre. No one had come to visit him. He sat sullenly by the window in his narrow room all day.

"Big writer, once. Harold Smith. Could scarcely believe it when I saw his file. No one's seen him in years," Ethel said, adjusting the tray of food in her hands.

Ethel was round and pale, with bright blue eyes and red hair that escaped from a bun to curl wildly around her face. She regularly slipped Roxanne titbits of gossip, seeming to know more even than Mrs. Cunningham.

"Sad, ain't it? Now they just drop 'im off here like a regular fellow."

Two days later, Roxanne went in Room 38 with an armful of fresh linen.

"Mr. Smith, I have to change the sheets."

He remained motionless in his chair.

"They said you have to get your dinner in the dining hall from now on."

She quickly stripped the sheets, then walked closer to look at him. His pale blue eyes seemed unfocused. Her pulse quickened. She had seen it done before, but had never had to check to see if someone had expired. She took a deep breath, gulped and began to reach out two fingers to his neck. Then, he blinked. She jumped and quickly ran back to the bed to put on the new white sheets.

As Roxanne fluffed the pillow, she noted the solitary picture on the night table of a cherub-pink face framed with wild curls.

"Is your granddaughter that?"

He didn't turn around.

"She's cute."

Roxanne balled up the dirty linen and began to head for the door.

"Are you from the Caribbean?" he said, turning his head slightly.

"Y-Yes." Roxanne started at the sound of his raspy voice.

"I remember the islands," he said simply, and turned back to the window. Roxanne waited, but that was all he said, so she crept from the room.

★

"He used to write crime stories," Ethel said through a mouthful of bread and jam.

Roxanne sat nursing her coffee in the staff lounge. "So, what happened?"

"Don't know, love," she said, "except that he stopped writing mysteries and started to write other stories that nobody could understand."

Roxanne downed the last of the coffee.

"Not one person comes to see him," Ethel said. "He just sits there. His son dropped him off that first time. They didn't say a word to each other."

Ethel got up and poured more tea into her mug.

"That's sad," Roxanne said quietly.

"Don't get too involved, lovey. First rule."

"I hope you plan to rejoin the workforce before noon."

They turned to find Madelaine Cunningham in the doorway. Although she was smiling, she was a formidable figure, standing there with sharp brown eyes magnified behind square-framed lenses.

Ethel shoved the last of the bread in her mouth and pushed back her chair. "C'mon, dear, before the dragon lady begins to spew fire."

"I heard that," Mrs. Cunningham said from halfway down the hall.

Roxanne hurried behind Ethel's waddling form.

★

"What's that you reading?"

Roxanne looked up to find Asha in the doorway, still wearing the apron from the restaurant down the street.

"Just something I got from the library. What's up?" She put aside the book, *The Other Side of Life* by Harold Smith and sat up.

"You wouldn't believe what I saw downstairs." Asha sat on the bed beside Roxanne, grinning.

"What?"

"Miss Carmen's got a man in the kitchen," Asha threw back her head, clapping her hands as she laughed. "You should have seen her face when I walked in. I think I interrupted something."

Roxanne chuckled. "I can't believe I didn't hear anything."

"They were standing close like they were kissing. When I walk in, she pushes him away like a schoolgirl in the boy's bathroom."

"No wonder I've not had to hear her stories, recently," Roxanne said, shaking her head.

"That's not the shocking thing."

"They were naked?"

Asha laughed again, patting her dark skin with the apron. "He's Indian."

"Miss Carmen?"

"I know. Shocking!"

"Stranger things have happened."

Roxanne was still shaking her head as Asha walked back to her room.

She lay back and picked up the book again. Ethel's

warning about not getting involved had only piqued her interest more and she'd headed to the public library to find out all she could about Harold Smith. There was precious little, only that he was born in Brixton, educated at Oxford, had one child in a brief marriage to a seamstress, Mavis Thornton, enjoyed some acclaim with the Inspector Radcliffe series, but became a recluse in 1982 after the poor public reception of his more serious fiction. She'd never cared much for crime thrillers, so had panned the twenty-four Radcliffe books for his last novel about an old man's solitary journey across the Atlantic Ocean. She had begun reading it on the train, but found it a difficult read with its dense paragraphs and difficult vocabulary. Yet, the thought of him sitting slouched by the window buoyed her.

She pulled the red bookmark from chapter five, then was suddenly doused in darkness. She heard a bump in the next room and Asha's angry mutterings in Swahili. She guessed they were very bad words.

A finger of light travelled into Roxanne's room and Asha was standing there in bra and shorts, shining a pen flash-light.

"She forgot to feed the meter?" Roxanne asked.

"I swear, one of these days – " Asha began.

"Sorry, loves." The singsong voice echoed up the stairs. "I'll take care of it."

Asha shone the penlight on the posters behind Roxanne. "Where's that?"

"It's Blue Lagoon in Portland," Roxanne said. "I can't believe all the places I haven't been in my own country."

"I know what you mean," Asha said. "When I went home last year, I travelled all over Nairobi because I had never left my village before coming here."

The lights came back on.

"That was quick," Roxanne said, picking up the book again.

"No doubt thanks to our Indian friend," Asha said, heading back to her room.

★

When Roxanne had a free moment before the end of her shift, she poked her head into Smith's room. He was bent over his bed.

"Mr. Smith, are you okay?"

He looked up toward the door but not directly at her.

"I… I…" How to begin? She struggled to get out the words. Having read his novel, she now saw him as someone with great intelligence and feeling. In the end, she'd been won over by the story and the main character's sheer gumption out there on the lonely seas.

"My grandfather used to work on a boat when he was young," she offered.

He looked away and climbed into bed. She began to walk away, then stopped.

"I used to love those trips to Old Harbour Bay too," she said. "Have you ever been to Jamaica?"

He looked up again and smiled slightly. From his picture on the dust jacket he must have been handsome once. Now, his face was a map of ridges and ravines, his bushy eyebrows and whiskers like muddy grey rushes.

"I went to Cuba once and to Trinidad," he rasped.

Roxanne smiled.

"Papa Jenkins always told us he would sail to Cuba before he died."

She brought the volume from behind her back.

"I tried to buy it, but they said it was out of print," she apologized. "I never thought I'd like a book about a stubborn old man and his dream to see the world."

He looked at the book. Then, he cocked his head and regarded her thoughtfully. "Do you think you could walk with me out to those willows outside? I figured that since I've seen them so much from this window, I should see them up close. My eyes don't work as well as they used to."

Roxanne took his left hand and he hobbled along with his right hand on his walker.

"So did he?" he said when they were outside.

"Who?"

"This Papa Jenkins."

"No. He died this year in his home in Red Ground."

"That's a pity," he said, "but it's just as well. A man can go mad if he finds that achieving his dream is not at all what he expected."

★

"That's the third time this week you stayed overtime, Roxanne," Ethel said, pulling on her jacket. "You know Cunningham will keel over before she pays you one extra cent, right?"

Roxanne put the towels on the top shelf of the closet and closed the door.

"I'm not doing it for the money, Ethel. I think I'm helping him."

Ethel was shaking her head. "Take it from me, love, it's always best to have some distance."

"Why d'you say that?" Roxanne asked. "I mean, nobody ever comes see him. What's the harm in that?"

Ethel put her large purse over her shoulder and regarded Roxanne for a moment.

"You seem determined to find out for yourself, dearie. Well, see you tomorrow. Don't let Cunningham get used to seeing you leave late. You'll never get back to your original time."

Ethel could really be annoying. Why was she going on like this? Her words ate away at the sense of usefulness Roxanne had nurtured over the past two weeks. She had enjoyed her little chats with Harold. It gave her a good feeling to see him open up.

"You have a curious sense of humour," he said when she'd found a topless page three girl from a 1978 newspaper in the main hall. She said she'd been tempted to post it on the bulletin board with a "Have You Seen My Owner" tag, just to see who would claim it when no one was around.

He had harrumphed in a way that she now realized wasn't annoyance but wry amusement.

"I guarantee by eight o'clock, someone will have taken it. I think is Lester own from Room 40," Roxanne offered. "He's been known to strip naked and wait for one of the female assistants to find him like that and then ask if she want 'sugar'."

"So, you think we are dead already, so why bother? You know it could very well be someone's wife here."

"I suppose so. The mystery of the page three girl," Roxanne had said, chuckling.

Their conversations had been like that, light and focused on his opinions of other residents and Roxanne's recollections of digging yam hills with Papa Jenkins.

One day, she brought in the third volume of the Inspector Radcliffe series and put it on the chair by his bed.

"I told you not to bring those in here," he grumbled.

"Don't you miss writing?" she asked.

"That was another time. I don't have much use for stories these days."

Roxanne sat down and flipped through the library copy. "Well, I can tell you now that I don't like who-done-its but this… this was… clever."

Harold had been harrumphing and Roxanne felt that this time it was in annoyance, but she decided to press on.

"You sound like my old school master," he said.

"Harold, why don't you want to talk about this adorable little girl in the photograph?"

Harold closed his eyes and fell silent.

"Okay then, Harold. I'll see you tomorrow. You should try to mingle with the others in the rec room. You're not a prisoner, you know. Stanley down the hall plays chess and he's always tryin' to show off."

"Call me 'Harry'," he said.

Roxanne smiled.

"Ok, Harry, I'll see you." She looked back at him. He appeared to be dozing.

As she closed the door, she glimpsed him open his eyes, reach for the photograph, and stroke the little face with a weathered hand.

★

Back in the apartment, pandemonium had broken out. Miss Carmen was sweeping up what sounded like broken glass in the kitchen, and Fiona was trying to get a curious brown stain out of a chair cushion.

"She was trying to make something for her Raj," Fiona whispered.

"Oh?" Roxanne was already heading for the staircase.

"Then, he called and said he was going back to his wife."

Roxanne stopped and looked back. She never thought she would actually feel anything but irritation for the woman. Now, she felt a faint prick of pity.

She continued up the stairs.

"Wait! We're going on a trip to Oxford this weekend. You want to tag along?"

"I was going to bring Harry some gizzada."

"Huh?"

"It's a pastry we make in Jamaica – a dough shell shaped like a starfish, well, a starfish with several legs, with a coconut centre –"

"Harry? You mean the old guy at the nursing home you keep talking about? I thought you weren't working this weekend."

"I'm not. I just want to show him something my granny taught me to make. We were talking about it the other day."

"You really hang around that place too much, Roxie. You need to meet some people your own age. Where's the secret lover?" Fiona laughed.

"Why you think I need a man? All man do is get you in trouble." Roxanne laughed, realising how easily her grandmother's words had fallen from her mouth.

"Saturday. Eight o'clock. Meet me downstairs," Fiona said, smiling.

★

How had she let herself be talked into this? The last time she'd been with Fiona and her group was on the tour of Leadenhall Market where scenes from *Harry Potter* had been filmed. This time, Fiona had brought along a fellow senior she was seeing, Barnaby Collingsworth the third. Asha had been inveigled into tagging along, too, and on the hourlong journey to Oxford she wondered to Roxanne why Fiona had insisted they come. It was so clearly Fiona and Barnaby's outing.

They didn't even get to sit together. Roxanne watched the twosome chattering at the front of the bus. Why hadn't she just made those gizzadas and taken them to Harold? Barnaby had been pleasant enough, and she couldn't say she disapproved of how Fiona's face lit up as the two chatted.

Now, she stood squinting at the little map she'd gotten from a bookstore, her cellphone long dead from all the web surfing on the bus.

Perhaps she should retrace her steps. Oxford had not been what she expected, save the old gothic buildings. Along almost every street, modern shops were squeezed in between them. She had been delighted to find a market that sold saltfish, scotch-bonnet pepper sauce, dried sorrel and tins of ackee imported from Jamaica. It was the crush of tourists she had not expected. Every second person she asked how to get back to the main street would brandish their own little map.

She'd better not stray too far in case the others came back for her. She was at the Canterbury Gate entrance of Christ Church. She would check out the picture gallery nearby while she waited.

Since she'd come, she had not ventured much outside London. She did not have what her father said were the wandering feet of her mother. But then she hardly knew her mother, had only one clear memory of her.

She remembered eating stewed jimbilines and running out into the rain with her, squishing water through galoshes while her father predicted they would both get ringworm and end up at the public hospital. Roxanne would close her eyes and see the jimbilines, brown and sticky and her mother's wide beautiful mouth, laughing and laughing.

Then she was gone, succumbed to pneumonia. Just like that. Roxanne was carted off to his parents' farm in Red Ground. She'd been sure then, at five, that she was to blame, that this frolic in the rain had killed her mother, not knowing about her mother's weak immune system.

As Roxanne entered the little gallery, a woman took her bag and the two-pound coin payment.

"No cameras. No touching, please," the woman said in what Roxanne now recognized as a Geordie accent.

Why did the women in these paintings look so stolid and sickly, whether wrapped in bundles of fabric or exposing milky round bodies? They were nothing like the market women back home in Liguanea, big brown women in colourful batiks, mouths bright and bellowing.

"Beautiful, isn't it?"

Roxanne turned to see a tall white man standing beside her.

Roxanne looked back at the painting of three figures, two women and a monk-like figure, the women both reaching to touch a baby.

"The Marriage of St. Catherine – said to be painted by Paolo Vernese in the sixteenth century," the man said, cleaning his glasses on his shirt.

"Is okay, I suppose." Roxanne looked at the women again, noting the same pallid, sombre look.

"Tough critic," the man said, laughing lightly.

Roxanne glanced back at him, noting the way the glasses highlighted his intense grey stare.

"Are you a tour guide?"

"Oh no. I teach over at Pembroke College. I just like coming here sometimes."

She looked at him, sceptical; he looked no older than she was – twenty-five.

"Where are you from?"

She sighed inwardly. The question so often led to some stranger's declaration that he or she had visited her country. She did not care to know another foreigner had seen parts of her country she had not.

"Jamaica," she said walking over to the other painting. The man followed.

"I thought so," he said. "I always liked that accent. As an undergrad, I went there to St. Ann to study ferns."

Roxanne smiled despite herself. Such a claim she had never heard before, but she pretended to look intently at the portrait of a woman staring in alarm out of the frame. Both she and the painted woman seeming to share the same unease, but she had paid her two pounds and intended to see every piece in this maze-like little gallery.

Finally, when he nodded at her and walked to the next room, Roxanne let out a little breath she hadn't realized she was holding.

She had better check for Fiona and the others. She collected her bag and came out of the gallery and looked around the courtyard to see if she could spot them. She wished she had written down their numbers instead of storing them in her useless phone, then at least she could find a payphone or a bistro willing to let her use the phone.

She sat on a bench near the gate before looking across and catching the eye of the man she had seen earlier. He was smoking a cigarette and Roxanne groaned when he dropped the butt, crushed it under his heel and came over. She reached into her bag and pulled out the next volume of the Inspector Radcliffe books she'd begun reading that morning.

"Hi again," he said.

"Hi," she said, just glancing at him.

"I'm Jeremy," he said, holding out a hand.

"Roxanne," she said, shaking his hand briefly and beginning to read her book.

"Oh, 'Roxanne', like that song by The Police?" He sat down beside her.

"The Police?" Roxanne turned over a page she had not read. She would give Fiona and the others half an hour and then she would take a bus back to London without them.

"You know, the song 'Roxanne'," he said, breaking into a few bars of the song: "Roxanne, you don't have to put on the red light. Those days are over. You don't have to sell your body to the nigh –"

"So, Roxanne is a whore?" she interrupted, pleased he'd gone so red. She laughed as he fumbled an apology.

"You like Harold Smith?" he asked, breaking the silence.

"What?"

He was pointing at the book.

"Oh… yes."

"Haven't seen those in ages. Met him once."

Roxanne looked up.

"You have?"

"Yes. As a kid, at a book signing in the eighties. I remember thinking he was mean-looking for someone whose books always made me laugh."

Roxanne closed the book, debating whether she should say she knew him.

The man took off his glasses and ran a hand through his hair. There was something interesting about his profile she had to admit.

"Sad what happened to his daughter-in-law and grand-daughter," he said.

"What's that?" Roxanne asked, the book forgotten in her lap.

"I remember seeing something in one of the papers," he said. "It was a little story. I only remember it because I thought it a shame they stuck it right next to the obituaries when he was such a big deal before."

Roxanne wished he would just get on with telling her what she had been trying to prise out of Harold for the past few weeks.

"Said it was his fault. Some said he'd been sloshed out of

his mind before he got behind the wheel," Jeremy said. "The little girl died instantly when he slammed into a tree, just five yards from his house. The daughter-in-law died in the ambulance."

"How long ago was this?"

"Eight, ten months ago," Jeremy said. "Such a shame. The little girl was only four."

Roxanne looked back at the book, studying the black and white photo of the younger Harold Smith.

"I've met him," she said. "I can't imagine how – "

"You have? Recently?" Jeremy asked.

"Yes. In London, at the nursing home where I work."

Roxanne looked up to find Fiona standing over her, with Barnaby and Asha close behind.

"Jesus H. Christ! We were scouring the city looking for you. Why the hell don't you answer your phone?"

Roxanne looked back at Jeremy. For the first time since she met him, she didn't want to get away from him.

"We were so worried and here you are quite comfy."

Roxanne had never known Fiona so cross.

"My phone died," Roxanne protested, "And this… this is Jeremy."

"How do you do?" Jeremy stood and extended his hand.

"Annoyed," Fiona grumbled, ignoring it.

Barnaby reached around Fiona and shook Jeremy's offending, outstretched hand.

"Let's go. We missed the trip to the Blenheim Palace," she said.

As Roxanne got up and began to put the book back in her bag, Jeremy reached for it and scribbled on the jacket flap under Harold's face.

"I'm coming to London next Monday. You can reach me here. I'd love to talk more… about Smith," he said.

Asha was grinning at her as Jeremy walked away.

★

Roxanne had thought of a hundred ways to introduce this new knowledge to Harold. He would be upset at first, but he would see she cared, that she at least did not condemn him.

When she entered the parking lot, she spotted the ambulance first and then, from where she stood, saw a few people in the gardens near Harold's favourite spot near the pines.

She raced around to where some residents were hovering and willed him not to be dead. She found another resident, Stanley, holding his left arm and howling.

Roxanne saw the overturned chess table and a dejected Harold sitting to one side, gripping his walking stick.

Roxanne began to move toward him when Ethel called her to help usher the residents back inside. She tried to get to Harold afterwards, but the manager, had taken him inside. It was half an hour before she found Harold sitting by the window in his room, with his son standing in the hallway, red-faced and thin-lipped, talking to Madelaine.

Before she could slip into the room, Roxanne felt a sharp tug and turned to find Ethel behind her. She pulled her into the laundry room.

"You really want to keep on interfering?"

"Is Stanley okay?" Roxanne asked. "What happened?"

"He broke his arm, love," Ethel said. "One minute they were playing chess peacefully and then your Harold struck Stanley with his cane."

Roxanne sighed. So it was "your Harold" and she was in some way to blame.

"Sit down, Roxanne," Ethel said. "Five years ago, there was this old woman here. She was dying. She was a DNR patient and I was not supposed to perform CPR on her. I had to beg for my job afterwards. I couldn't just let her die. Just a few minutes before she was telling me how her husband would never forget the name of his young nurse, but hardly knew who she was, his wife of forty-eight years. Then, she was on the floor gripping her chest and was unconscious in seconds. I rushed to pump her chest and give her mouth-to-mouth."

"So did she die?"

"Oh no. She lived. That was the problem. The paramedics came and three weeks later the family sued the home because I broke a rib trying to save her life."

Roxanne looked back along the corridor to where Madelaine was still speaking animatedly with Harold's son.

"And they won, Roxanne," Ethel said, turning Roxanne around and grasping her shoulders. "No matter how much we care about them, they are not our family."

When Ethel released her and left the room, Roxanne stood there letting the feeling of dread pool in her chest. What could she say to him now? She had pressed him to make friends with the residents. She had all but put the chess pieces in his hand.

When she entered the hallway again, Madelaine was leading Harold's son back to her office. Roxanne hesitated for a moment, then slipped into the room where Harold was still slumped near the window.

"Is… is he dead?" he asked before Roxanne could say a word.

"Ethel says you broke his arm." Roxanne sat on the edge of the bed and waited for him to continue.

"He called me a child killer."

"I know what happened… to your granddaughter and your daughter-in-law," Roxanne said.

He was silent for a moment.

"That awful night," he said quietly. "My little Emily, and Sarah… just gone." He was holding a photo, of the child, she guessed.

"I had stopped drinking for a whole week before the accident. I was taking them home on Christmas Eve. Emily said, 'Granddad. Look! For the Christmas tree!' So I looked… and then we were spinning. I still remember the awful crunching sound it made when the car slammed into that tree. When I opened my eyes, the first thing I saw was the paper ornament. It was perfect. Unscathed. Sitting on dashboard like she had just carefully placed it there. Then I looked back at Emily… Her eyes were open and the blood was everywhere. Sarah was screaming and screaming, suspended above her. I see it all the time."

They sat there in silence for a moment.

"Harry, I'm sorry." She was thinking of her mother, her father, her grandmother, and especially her grandfather, Papa Jenkins. All gone. She knew loss, but to have one's family taken all at once at one's own hand, was unimaginable.

"I didn't mean to hit Stanley," Harold said after a long pause. "I didn't mean…"

"I'm so sorry, Harry. There was nothing you could do –"

"Mr. Smith, your son is here."

Roxanne turned to find Madelaine standing there in the room, Harold's stony-faced son in tow.

"Ms. Jenkins, please get back to your duties," she said evenly.

Roxanne rose slowly. Harold had his head turned away.

"Ms. Jenkins!" Madelaine said more forcefully.

As Roxanne pulled the door behind her, she paused to cast Harold a parting look. He offered a weak smile. He looked ravaged by loss, but there was something else, like relief on his face.

This would probably be the last time she saw him. It was not her business. He was not her father. He was a patient in this foreign place she worked. His loss was not her loss, but why did she feel this way?

Perhaps Ethel was wrong.

★

When she had finished attending to the other residents, she returned to Harold's room to find it empty, the bed stripped, the photograph gone.

She went to the chair facing the view of the pines. There was something comforting about it.

"Ah, here you are!" Madelaine's reflection filled up the window "Aren't you going home?"

"Am I fired?" Roxanne asked quietly.

"Why would I fire you?"

"The incident... with Harry ... um ... Mr. Smith."

"You weren't on duty, and you can't control the actions of the residents... Should I fire you for something?"

Roxanne shook her head.

"Was your relationship with Mr. Smith inappropriate in some way?"

"Inappropriate?"

"Did he make... advances?" Madelaine cleared her throat uncomfortably.

"No. Of course not!"

"Good... good," she said, briskly. "We don't need any more legal trouble."

Before Madelaine left the room, she turned and said, "Oh, he left this for you." She held out a book to Roxanne. "I thought it was his copy, but he says it's yours."

Roxanne took her beaten-up library copy of *The Other Side of Life*.

"Left? Is he going somewhere?"

"His son is taking him to another home until all this can be sorted out. Now, please go home, Ms Jenkins. It's past six o'clock."

"Yes, ma'am," Roxanne said to Madelaine's retreating back. She looked down at the book. As she got up, a note fell out. She unfolded it:

"*Story? Papa Jenkins. West Indian. Sees Cuba for the first time. Granddaughter. Beautiful young woman. Petulant. Inquisitive. Compassionate.*"

Roxanne read again what must be Harold's handwriting and felt a smile forming. She looked at the view of the pines, turned and walked from the room.

FINDING JOY

Ayo looked out at the cypress trees drooping over the lake in the middle of campus, a place that had once brought her some semblance of peace. She watched an alligator slice its way through the ripples of mossy-green water. She touched a hand to her stomach.

When would it bleed away? It had been hours since she drank the concoction. She had been restless waiting for it to work, and her roommate Sarah had kept asking her what the matter was, so she'd walked out to stand by the lake.

Back home in Jamaica, girls who fell pregnant were rumoured to travel long distances to seer women or men up in the mountains of St. Thomas or St. Mary. There was talk of cerasee bush, wild cassava, and various strange oils, but whatever was said or done in secret Ayo did not know. She just knew you never saw any growing bellies on those girls from respectable churchgoing families upon their return from up country to Spanish Town.

She only had the college library here and a limited supply of ingredients – wild bitter melon, one book had said; another, unripe papaya and cinnamon. Wild passion flower? Where would she find that in the grocery aisle? Primrose oil, wild tansey and sesame seeds? In the end, back in her dorm room, she had crushed sesame seeds and a whole green papaya with the butt of a knife and boiled the leaves of a wild bitter melon teabag with cinnamon in her portable kettle and downed it in two chunky gulps. It was more pleasant than she had thought. Maybe it needed to be vile to work, like cod-liver oil or the black castor oil her mother forced her to take for "wash-outs" every month.

An abortion clinic would be a public acknowledgment of her failings. It would be like asking her Auntie to mount her on a pyre in the middle of church grounds and have them chant her sins until she was reduced to ash.

No, she would have to wait for it to work.

She looked out at the turtles sunning themselves on a piece of bark. The half-submerged alligator seemed to peer at her, condemning her for wishing the thing gone from her body.

She had been in Louisiana for just six months. She had thought, given its proximity to the Caribbean, it would feel more like home than New York, though more of her distant relatives had settled there.

But the brick buildings in this sleepy college town, the white faces, the Southern drawl, the strange way they said "crayfish" like "paw" instead of "pay", still made her miss the patch of land in St. Mary where her uncle reaped pak choy, bananas and corn and petted the East Indian trees that gave him fat, meaty mangoes in the summer time. How disappointed he would be if he knew what she had done.

A light breeze tossed her short curls and cooled her damp face. She was grateful no one had come by when she let the tears flow. She watched a cyclist appear and disappear like a haunting through the hanging grey cypress leaves.

The lake in the middle of a university campus had been her oasis. She would sit on a bench and watch the squawking birds fly from tree to tree. If she closed her eyes she could imagine she was out by the river in Port Maria, sinking stones with her cousins, stealing cashews from private land and fishing janga from the river – in that golden time before she had to move from her grandmother's house.

They had moved when her uncle and her mother could no longer agree on the division of labour, and since the land had passed to her uncle and not to her mother, they had to leave. They ended up in Spanish Town, far from open fields and large bodies of water save the winding Rio Cobre. Her mother thought she would find better-paying work in the city, but Spanish Town proved as disappointing for them both as Ayo was finding Louisiana now.

When she had first come alone to the lake, sitting far from the other students who had come to chat and read, she felt she could endure whatever lay ahead. Now things had changed and not even the lake could assuage her shame.

★

Growing up in that Spanish Town garrison community, she'd longed to escape back to the open fields of Port Maria, away from zinc fences and asphalt, away from gun fire and curfews. During election time, she learned to hide herself. Her school uniform of green gingham and gabardine – the colour of the Labour party – was now like a death wish in a community brandishing their affiliation to the People's party in bright orange. She knew to jump into a ditch when she heard the sound of gunshots and saw the police in battle gear. Then, she'd sprint to her tenement and learn whether she could leave for school the next day. At the time, she had never dreamed of America. Going there seemed as improbable as going to outer space. The lucky few she knew who went, did not come back the same – if they came back at all.

Her fantasy was to live in the quiet, upscale neighbourhoods in St. Andrew, where she knew her father must live with his "real" family.

Her mother wouldn't talk about him. His very existence was obscured by myth and silence. Ayo knew her bastard status too well. She was the daughter of a banker for whom her mother had worked as a domestic helper – that was all.

"You could have had a whole other life, Yo-yo," her uncle had said, the day they began harvesting the corn when she was not yet ten. "The best of everything money could-a buy, baby love."

She had asked what he meant, but he said nothing as he looked out of the window at his sister battling with the prickly branches of the cherry tree.

"Is like the story our granny used to tell us about the woman and the giant python," he said, patting her head and smiling. "The story say how the snake wash himself in a river and transform into a man, and charm him way into the woman house, and when she let him inside, he turn back into a snake and wrap himself around the house and his mouth full up the doorway, so the only way out was for her to let him eat her up."

"That's a silly story," she had said, giggling.

"Is a story that come from our West African ancestors, Yo-yo. It's just as good as the stories they tell you at school about the red coats and fat English kings. Don't never forget that."

Her uncle's stories were often hard to decipher – stories about big bullfrogs captured by tiny fire ants or why no matter how tall the sugar cane grew it could not blot out the sun – but she came back to this woman and python again and again, especially when she saw a picture of her father in the newspaper the year she turned fifteen.

He grinned back at her from the singed newsprint photo, looking serpentine. He was wearing a tuxedo, standing beside a light-skinned woman in white. She had learned bits and pieces over the years to explain why her complexion was more caramel than her mother's dark coffee, why she had hazel eyes and not her mother's dark brown, why she had big curls instead of kinks, and why there wasn't even one picture of her father – any father – in the house. She felt a strange mix of relief and anger looking at a face so much like her own.

If her mother had not ripped up the page with the announcement of the marriage, wadded it into a ball and tossed it into the open coal stove outside, perhaps Ayo would not have cared enough to rescue it from the flames with a stick. She looked at the woman on his arm, her body swaddled in white silk or satin or chiffon and wanted to ask her mother more.

"Might as well you know, child."

Her mother had come up behind her. "That the man who put you inside me, and that is the second whore he marry in twelve years. Some people not worth your energy. We can leave them only to Jehovah. Now go and sweep out the front room."

"Mama, why –"

"Go and sweep out the front room," was all she would say, and that was it.

★

It was her high school English teacher, Ms. Evans, who planted America as escape in Ayo's mind. Until then she had been content to sit at the back of the fourth-form class and look out through the louvre blades, counting the hours until she could be set free on the savannah.

She did not scream at her mother, ditch school, run away, or go to the place where her father lived with his second wife. She settled instead for a deadening melancholia. She would allow herself to be buffeted by whatever might come.

"Ayo! Apply yourself more," Ms. Evans urged. "Stop doodling and daydreaming in my class."

Ms. Evans might as well have howled at the moon for all the good it did – at first. One day, though, she pulled Ayo aside and showed her SAT booklets and told her that while she prepared for the local GCE and the CXC exams, she could also prepare for the American tests.

"You used to do so well," she said. "You can be that way again. You can become somebody over there. I see it in you, Ayo."

Ms. Evans made America sound like another planet, where she would have anything she wanted, where no one would care if she had a father or not, where she could be anything she wanted, not a country girl trying to make a life in the city with a mother who no longer believed that anything could be achieved in this world, who sought only redemption from God.

Ayo started to imagine how the two-room house that she shared with her mother, with the second-hand furniture and the crisscrossing power lines that brought them stolen electricity, must look through Ms. Evans's eyes. She had to escape. She began to apply herself.

When she completed sixth form, when Ms. Evans excitedly told her she had been offered part-scholarships to colleges in Florida, Louisiana, Virginia, and New York, Ayo had felt something akin to triumph, but undercut by the dread of having to tell her mother.

It was as she expected.

"So Miss Evans is you mother now? I have a mind to go tell her fi mind her own dyamn business. And who tell you to bring that lady hereso?"

Ayo endured the litany of her mother's rant as they watched Ms. Evans step over rusting car parts in the yard, a group of women braiding each others' hair eyeing her suspiciously.

Perhaps Ms. Evans had thought that all she had to do was cast America in the glow she had done before with Ayo and her mother would concede. Her mother listened to Ms. Evan's calm explanations of how Ayo could be successful, return to Jamaica one day and take them out of their present circumstances.

"Think how when she comes back she can have a better job –"

"Than selling fruit like me?" Ayo's mother said hotly.

"Well… yes, Mrs. Richards," Ms. Evans said.

Ayo noticed her mother did not correct the use of the title she did not have.

"And who paying this money, ma'am?"

"The university over there pays eighty percent, and I will organize something so the school can help with embassy paperwork," Ms. Evans said. "It's a great opportunity. And Ayo can join work-study over there."

Ayo had stood near the doorway silently watching her mother, willing her not to destroy her one chance.

"Well… Since as me outnumbered," her mother said finally, in a tone of surrender. "But she should pick the Louisiana school. My half-sister, Gene, she live in Breaux Bridge last I hear."

In the beginning, it had felt like the escape Ayo had prayed for, but quite rapidly she knew she had swapped one bondage for another.

In Aunt Gene's house Ayo had to follow her aunt's puritanical edicts, where everything not of the church was "evil" and "of the devil". When it wasn't mandatory bible study every Sunday and Wednesday, she was up to her elbows in suds and scrubbing pads with her Aunt's constant reminder: "Cleanliness is next to godliness" reverberating in her brain.

"Yes, I will make sure she go church, Charmaine," Ayo had heard Auntie Gene tell her mother shortly after arriving. "Yes, I will make sure that this school don't corrupt 'er. Yes. Don't worry 'bout nothing. God still on His throne."

This was why she had courted trouble and searched for reasons to live in the dorms rather than suffer any more of her Aunt's holy household.

"I can be more involved in the prayer groups they have on campus, Auntie," Ayo had said. "They have all kinds of Christian groups there. I have come to see that this is a very Christian, godly place, Auntie."

She had no intention of joining any group, but with the promise to show Auntie Gene religious literature from the groups – to "make sure them wasn't from the devil" – Ayo moved into the dormitories.

★

Perhaps if she had sat on the other side of Cypress Lake in the second month of the semester, she would have avoided him altogether, and Auntie Gene's prophecies about the ills that could befall her unsupervised niece on the college campus would not have come to fruition.

Ayo had been reading *The Sound and The Fury* for English credit, eating a sandwich on the bench near the lake one day, when she looked over and found a man staring at her from a nearby bench. He looked a little older than she was, at least twenty-five or twenty-six, white, slender, with thick dark hair. He was wearing a blue, collared shirt and khaki slacks. When he smiled at her, she snapped her head back to the pages of the book.

"One time, they escaped," he said quite loudly.

"Excuse me?" she said, squinting over at him.

He got up and came to stand next to her, pointing to the alligators that had climbed on the muddy bank nearby, just beyond the fencing.

"Last semester. An alligator and a giant snapping turtle. Right where you're sitting."

Ayo flinched and he chuckled.

"I'm kidding," he said, laughing a little louder.

"About them escaping or where they escaped to?" She looked anxiously at the immobile reptiles on the muddy bank a stone's throw away.

"No. They did escape. We put them back. It was the other side, near that brick wall, though."

"We?"

"I'm in the biology department. They ran a feature on it on the 5'oclock news when it happened. Didn't you see it? A real spectacle."

"No," Ayo said. "It's my first semester."

"I'm Forrest," he said. "Can I sit here?"

He sat before she could object.

"I'm Ayo."

"Ahh… yoh" he said, elongating both syllables of her name reverently, like a prayer. "That's pretty."

"It… it means 'Joy' in Yoruba," she said, not knowing what else to say. Her mother had not known this fact, Ayo knew, when she gave her the name. It had been a name that swirled about when her mother worked in the banker's house and somehow it had stuck. Learning its meaning had been accidental – when she found out about a singer with the same name, while doing a research assignment on Nigeria in high school.

"I like your accent. Where in Africa are you from?"

Ayo laughed, despite her uneasiness.

"It's an African name, yes, but I'm from Jamaica."

"Oh! My parents went to Montego Bay for their second honeymoon."

Ayo looked back over at the lake. The alligators had swum back to its centre and climbed onto the makeshift ramp there. What an easy life they must have. Nothing to do but swim and eat and rest. The breeze brought his scent to her, reminding her of something from back home – citrus, wood, lemon grass, sea water…

"Do you like it?" he asked.

"Like what?" She wondered if he could have possibly read her mind.

"Do you like Lafayette?"

She paused. Many strangers had asked her that question – cashiers, bus drivers, the maintenance man, her resident advisor, her roommate, Sarah, and she had learned she could not answer with a quick and curt "no" without injuring someone. The question usually had a follow-up, expressed with varying degrees of curiosity – or barely concealed concern – about when she would return to Jamaica. To this she never gave the same answer.

"It's… okay," she amended now. "It grows on you, I suppose."

"What's that? Chicken?" he asked, pointing to her half-eaten sandwich.

She lifted the top slice of bread to reveal the little golden-brown slabs.

"It's plantains. We fry them back home. Ripe ones and even the green ones," she said. "These… these are ripe ones."

Frying them in her dorm room on a contraband hot plate had not been easy, but she did not tell him this. She looked back at him and for a moment forgot her nervousness. She noted how animated his features were. His whole face seemed to smile as she talked about it, about how one slightly crushed green plantains to make them like chips to eat with any protein dish, or how you sliced ripe plantains and how the overripe ones would caramelize and burn at the edges, which was the best kind because it became like candy – and how she found this a quick way to keep homesickness at bay.

The few times she had looked back at him while she babbled away, she could not make out if his eyes were steel grey or ice blue, and the intent way he stared at her when he was listening only increased her unease.

"Maybe we could have lunch right here tomorrow afternoon," he was saying. "And maybe you could fix some of those plantains for me?"

"Okay," she said, before she could think about it fully.

"And we eat plantains here, too," he said with a smile. "Just like you described."

Ayo smiled at the way he said "plantains" like "maintains" instead of like back home how they said it like "mountains".

"I'll be here around this time as usual," she managed to say as he walked away.

Did he mean they were to eat lunch side by side or did he mean he would meet her there and did she need to wear something nice and was it a date?

She watched a group of girls wave at him.

And did they just call Forrest, Professor Thibodeaux?

★

Forrest did return the next day, and Ayo discovered he was, in fact, thirty-two years old and was not a "real professor" but "just" a postgraduate student teaching some undergraduate credits. She did, however, come to feel less strange about it as time went on, buoyed by his humour and his easy way with her. They met there the next day and the next and the next.

She began to lie awake in bed while her roommate, Sarah, wheezed in sleep a few feet away, and think about him. Every boy at her high school had given her a wide berth because of her "Ms. Christian" mother who sold fruits and bag juice at the school gate, which Ayo knew was partly to keep an eye on her. So, here she was, nineteen, and never even been kissed.

She remembered one night when she was about eleven years old and they had just moved to the Spanish Town house. She had heard a curious moaning on the other side of the fence and peeked through a hole in the galvanized zinc at gyrating naked bodies. Before she knew what had happened, she felt the sting radiate across her cheek, and then she was being pulled by her ear back to the house. She looked up in bewilderment at her enraged mother who launched into a long rant about iniquity, pleasures of the flesh, and grasping men who would only want to take her virtue.

Some of the girls at her school, as young as twelve, had boasted about having sex with older men in the community, but the only direct sex education Ayo had gotten was when her thirteen-year-old classmate, Oliver "Big Boy" Hutchinson, took out his semi-erect member, right there under the mango tree in the school yard and showed her.

"Me jus' cock it up like so, and then me jus' push it in yuh pum-pum," he said, matter-of-factly. "Mek me show you."

But as he moved toward her, Ayo bolted with hands outstretched and flailing, her shrieks loud and long as though she had just spotted the fabled rolling calf.

The easy way it happened, her first kiss with Forrest, had made her feel less apprehensive about any other physical intimacy that might come in their relationship. Their lunches had graduated to other places around campus and then to places downtown. This went on for a few weeks before, one day, as they walked across campus, she stopped him to point at the looming trees with the large blooming white flowers and asked him what was the big deal about magnolia trees in the South, how she had seen the reference *ad nauseum* in almost every Southern text she had to read for her English class, but she never got an answer. When she looked back at him, his eyes were lingering at her mouth, and suddenly he pressed his lips against hers right there in public. She had bristled more in surprise than revulsion, but as he angled his head and deepened the kiss, she knew then why her mother had warned her. The more his mouth mated with hers, the more she wanted the warmth to spread through her whole body.

After that, Ayo knew it was impossible to ignore what she was feeling or to cast it off as mere flirtation. He consumed her thoughts, and her time with Forrest was like the smooth blue-black stones she collected back in Port Maria when she was five and still lived on her uncle's land with her mother and her cousins. Over and over, she turned them in her mind, even as she sat in class: the smell of his starched shirt, his warm tongue, his fingers on the small of her back, the heat threading through her body, the taste of his mouth.

One day, when she could not bear it anymore, Ayo fibbed her escape from Auntie Gene, whom she had promised to see during Spring Break, telling her that she had been chosen to complete a special interim project at school and needed to spend the vacation on campus. Instead, she went to see Forrest.

He took her to his apartment. Somehow, she had expected to see clothes strewn everywhere, books piled high on the counter near to the stove, food remnants crusting the microwave door, dirty dishes submerged in cold, soapy water in the sink. This had been how Sarah described some of the rooms of her male friends on campus. Even Ayo's uncle had been known to trudge fresh mud through the house in his water boots, just as her mother had waxed the floor, even used a coconut husk to bring it to a brilliant shine.

Forrest's apartment was pristine.

"It's so clean," she said, and he laughed.

"We aren't all slobs."

As he chatted about how long he had lived in the apartment and joked about the hoof-like steps of the tenants above him, she could feel the charged energy between them.

She felt like a child in her fear, but when they stood in the narrow passageway leading to his bedroom, she found herself pressing her palm against his mouth when he tried to tell her another meaningless fact about the aging pipe system and nodded to his unspoken request.

Pulling her hand away, feeling wild in her nervousness, she stepped back from him and pulled at the buttons on her dress. She looked up at him, relishing how his gaze followed the descending path of her fingers.

She had scarcely let the dress fall to the floor, when he closed the gap between them and gruffly kissed her. She thought absently that she didn't know his middle name, nor his birth stone, and that it was only four weeks since he'd been talking to her about escapee amphibians. He made her feel wanted and wanton and reckless.

But, in the midst of their frenzy, when they had gotten to the bed somehow, and she lay there naked before him, looking up at his pale body kneeling before her on the bed, and feeling the heat pulse through her abdomen, she swore she saw her mother appear at the foot of the bed in her Sunday best, her praise tambourine raised high in her hand. Ayo jumped.

"What's wrong?" he asked, following her gaze behind him towards the empty doorway.

"Nothing… Nothing…" She shook her head and turned on her side.

He lay next to her and pulled her against him and she gasped at the pressure of his arousal against her thigh.

"Are you sure?" he whispered, running a hand down the length of her body and kissing the nape of her neck.

"Is… is my first time," she said, closing her eyes and burying her face in the pillow.

She felt him turn her over; her eyes searched his and found his gaze reassuring. No real surprise registered in his face at her confession. Had it been so obvious?

"I will be gentle," he murmured, kissing her bottom lip. "I promise."

He moved away from her and she watched him secure a condom. She glanced back at the emptiness at the foot of the bed and felt foolish about her misgivings.

She felt his warm hands on her breasts and savoured the feeling, and when his hands slid down her body and parted her legs, she opened to him, and bit her lip as he stroked her.

Then a bible text flashed through her mind. *For a whore is a deep ditch and a strange woman is a narrow pit.* She tossed her head from side to side, trying to shake away the words, but another came to her.

Repent and turn yourselves from all transgressions, so iniquity shall not be your ruin.

She was moaning in her dual torment, but she didn't ask him to stop and Forrest's breathing became more laboured and his stroking more ardent. He was hovering over her, and she knew what it meant to lose herself. She knew she had to let it happen.

"Don't be nervous," he said, and Ayo reached up impulsively, threaded her hand through his hair and pulled him down for a kiss and then her mouth broke from his as she cried out when she felt the pressure of his body entering hers and it was like an elastic band stretched and burst inside her as he began to move.

When she opened her eyes she saw Auntie Gene this time, shaking the tambourine over her head and chanting: *"Sinner! Fornicator! Repent! Repent!"* as Forrest began rocking deeper and deeper.

She closed her eyes tight and held onto him and willed away the fire and brimstone messenger, and let her body give into its want. Even in the pain of his thrusting, there was something wonderful building inside her, but then it stopped as Forrest tossed his head back, held unto her hips, shuddered and collapsed against her, panting.

Ayo lay there running a hand through his sweat-drenched hair, wondering how anyone could call what had just happened between them evil. Her mother had always said that people who gave in to the pleasures of the flesh would suffer the hottest part of hell for all eternity.

"How do you feel?" he asked, quietly, when his breathing became more even.

Ayo opened her mouth, but no words came out.

He moved back and propped his head up with his arm and regarded her intently.

She looked at him and gave him a sad smile.

"Are you sorry?" he asked.

Ayo thought about it for a moment.

"No," she said, "Not at all."

"Good," he said, with a slow, languid smile.

"But…" she said, "I don't think I was… well, it felt like … but then, it didn't happen…"

"That was my fault," he said quietly, with a sheepish smile.

Then he rolled over and pulled her on top of him. "But we could try again."

He cupped her buttocks.

"…and again…"

She giggled despite herself.

"…and again…"

"I have to go home soon," she said. "But maybe, maybe just one more time…"

"You may need to give me a moment, though," he said, laughing.

Later that evening, she glanced at Forrest's sprawled naked form on the bed beside her and marvelled at how stark his pale skin was against hers, and an old fear surged through her.

She remembered her mother and the pain she must have endured breaking the rules trying to enter her father's world, but she thought it was mainly because her father was cruel and not because he was a white man.

A short while after arriving in Lafayette, Ayo realized she had begun to think about herself in a way she had not done before. The first time she realized this was when she moved around the aisles of the Piggly Wiggly and found the same man following her, first in the cereal aisle, then the beans aisle, then even by the feminine products. And was the cashier a germophobe or did she just did not want to touch her outstretched hand, instead dropping the change into it from far above? Were these misgivings not mere imaginings? No one had spat in her face or called her a nigger.

She knew, most of all, that her mother would not understand, though both she and her Auntie Gene would see Forrest as a heathen first, before anything else.

Things were different back home. There, people prided themselves on being black, East Indian, Maroon, or Chinese. There she rarely thought of her black skin as now she did in America. Of course, even in her black majority country, there was always the reminder of their colonization by the British crown in the small percentage of whites, like her absentee father, who were usually the "haves" who held positions of power and privilege, as if it was a right, who distanced themselves from the "have nots". People with dark complexions still had to have some measure of hard-won success and prestigious education to live along side them.

Here, she knew the twisted history of separation between people was more clearly tied to skin colour and not so much to class, and while she saw some interracial couples, she knew that intolerance still lurked just beneath the surface. She saw it in the furtive glances black and white students alike gave them when she and Forrest walked on campus, arms linked; she heard it in the offensive jokes about black women and their insatiable sexual appetites; she felt it in her discomfort when Forrest kissed her in public.

She could not help herself. She felt intoxicated with her need to be with him, even if he could never understand her world. Why could she not talk to him about why she felt out of place in classrooms where only a few others looked like her and fewer still sounded like her?

Now, she reached out and moved a lock of his hair over his forehead and then began to move away from him until his arm reached out and stayed her.

"Don't go. Stay the night," he said, his eyes still closed, as he brought her back down against him.

"I can't."

He sighed and sat up, pulling the sheet around them.

"You are not a child, Ayo," he murmured.

"I know, but…"

"Then stay."

"You don't understand," she said. "My Auntie likes to call the dorm to make sure I'm there, especially when I don't go to her house during these breaks."

Her bare feet touched the carpet, and the soft bristles against her soles seemed to bring her out of her haze of contentment. She wondered if she would ever be the same again and if she could hide what had happened from her Auntie when she saw her again.

Did she look like those girls men said were womanly, who swayed their hips differently now that they knew all? Was it a thing that people could see in her face, in the way she moved? Could they tell she was no longer pure?

She tried not to look back at him as she slipped on her dress, nor linger when he kissed her goodbye at the door.

But then, she stopped with her hand on the doorknob.

"What does this mean? What do I call you now?"

"What do you mean?" he asked, his brows knitting.

"Never mind," she said, gave him another quick kiss, and fled.

★

After that first night, it was a marvel she could keep her mind on her studies. For several weeks, she had woken up in his bed and had even brought her books with her in the misguided belief that she would study. It baffled her how he seemed able to prepare for his teaching day, or work on his research, while she felt content to lie beside him, spent, listening to the muted clicks of his computer. She would busy herself arranging things in his apartment and he, patiently at first, would answer her questions about the odds and ends in his home.

Yet, whenever they were apart for more than a few hours, he seemed just as urgent for her to return to him as she did.

One evening, while she took the last shift at the cafeteria, she looked up to find Forrest standing outside, just mere hours after she had left his bed. It only took one look before she stole away. In moments, they were flush against the bathroom stall, and she had one hand over his mouth, the other braced against the door and both legs curled around his naked thighs.

If she was going to hell for this, she would go in a spectacular fireball of ecstasy, she thought, as she moved against him.

★

In the weeks following this, Ayo revelled in bliss that was foreign to her. Joy tinged with worry. She tried not to let the uneasiness form itself fully inside her, to spread through her like a virus while she sat across from Forrest in a café, or in his lab, or at the spot where they first met. She tried not to analyse his every facial expression. Yet, if his brows furrowed, momentarily, she worried she had said something to displease him. When he became sombre and did not speak for a while, she would reach out and touch him as though in this way she could transfuse reassurance of her devotion from her body to his.

She imagined their every lull as a pulling away.

She silently cursed her mother for this inherited mistrust of happiness. *Is jus a matter of time*, she could almost hear her mother say, like the saying she used to drum into her like a warning – *Chicken merry, Hawk deh near.*

Her uncle told of how the chicken hawk became predator and the hen his prey. Hawk and Hen went into the wilderness to find a strong guango tree to make a drum. They cut it down together and formed the drum and put it in the sun to dry. Hawk told Hen not to touch it until he returned with victuals, but Hen was too impatient, and when Hawk had been long on his journey to find them food, Hen pulled the drum into the shade and beat it three times. So enamoured was she with the sound that she beat it again and again. Hawk could hear it where he was and became enraged. Hen did not hear as Hawk approached, lost in her jaunty little song. She did not know Hawk had returned until she felt Hawk's beak rip through her neck.

"Did you hear me?" Ayo found herself saying more often to Forrest as the semester wore on.

She said it now as she looked at him across from her in the library.

"What?" He took off his glasses and rubbed his eyes.

"Never mind," she said, picking up her own notebook and highlighting a random word.

When she looked back at him, he seemed so genuinely lost that she immediately forgave him. Of course, he should be more interested in his research than what she had just said about how much she missed home, that she missed the time she was a child on her uncle's farm when the cassavas were as big as her head, and her uncle would tell her stories about Anancy she had not heard at school.

She longed to talk to someone who would understand. Her roommate, Sarah, listened but, somehow, it was just not as gratifying telling her. Sarah was a pleasant, round, blond girl from New Iberia who had greeted her with a tight hug the moment Ayo entered their dorm room that first day. She was easy to like. Yet, Sarah did not have Forrest's capacity to listen. She always interrupted with questions before Ayo could finish her story – about what tamarinds were, or star-apples, or whether Jamaica had national parades as Louisiana had during Mardi Gras.

"I'm sorry, babe," Forrest had said, squeezing her hand. "You know my conference is coming up. Haven't even written a word of the paper yet. Can we talk about it tonight?"

"Sure," Ayo said. "I should be studying anyway."

How could she bear a whole week without him? Why didn't he seem as anxious about their parting as she did?

When he looked over his book at her and smiled, Ayo smiled back, trying to subdue the sick feeling of dread at the pit of her stomach.

★

The way she discovered that she had a problem came through Sarah.

The girl had come bounding into their dorm room, one afternoon, her face red from running and her blond hair escaping from her ponytail.

"Can I borrow a tampon? Oh my god, how embarrassing. I can't believe this happened to me. Everybody in class saw, oh god!"

Ayo took one look at her sweater tied around her jeans like a skirt and understood. Then the realization came like a sudden tightness spreading through her chest, that in the two and a half months since she'd begun to have sex with Forrest, she had only had her period once. Quick math told her she was at least fourteen days late.

"Well, can I? I'm out."

Perhaps she was now on Sarah's cycle.

"Ayo!"

Ayo nodded absently and pointed to their shared bathroom, barely containing the panic raging through her.

And when Ayo had been sure, after she used five pregnancy tests from Walgreens with all her remaining pay, and sank to the grimy floor of their bathroom in tears, she wondered how easily she had become the very thing her mother had spent all her childhood warning her against.

★

A few days before he was to leave for his conference, Ayo went to visit Forrest in the department and he had smiled and waved at her from his stool.

What she had to tell him would not be welcome news. How soon would he lose his smile when he saw how this would disrupt all their lives?

His female colleague looked over at her and smiled.

Did she hear the woman giggle as she whispered to Forrest: "This one is a little young, isn't she?"

Perhaps she had misheard. Still, her mind echoed back her doubts: Did he find this woman more suitable? They were probably the same age – not a mere undergraduate. She had pale skin like him, and red curly hair and probably understood all his complex science jokes and how to pay attention to her body so as not to find herself in the situation she now found herself.

Then Forrest looked at Ayo in a way that made her know he still desired her. The nagging voices went quiet for a while.

They would just have to deal with this together. It would be fine. She was not unique. At least three girls in her high school had left when their uniform tunics could no longer disguise swollen bellies, and at least one now had her own haberdashery in St. Jago Plaza.

It would be fine.

It was not the end of the world.

"You ready for lunch?" Forrest asked.

Ayo nodded.

When his colleagues – two men along with the redhead – tagged along, Ayo felt the panic building again. She sat across from them, feeling herself diminished by the assured way they talked. The sandy-haired one with the square lens and polo shirt and the Indian one with the Rip-Van-Winkle-like beard debated with Forrest and Brenda about the climatic adaptations of sea life.

Ayo played with the salt and pepper shakers, trying not to succumb to the wave of nausea rippling through her.

"I am deathly afraid of sea turtles," she murmured, when they had stopped talking. "My Uncle Merville's so afraid of swimming in the ocean."

She looked up to see them looking at her as though she had just spoken in a different language.

"That's so... interesting," the red-haired colleague, Brenda Something said, in a way Ayo felt one would speak to a confused child.

Forrest patted Ayo's hand and downed a spoonful of his soup. Perhaps in the beginning it would have reassured her, but now it felt condescending, like a silencing.

"So, are you guys, official?" Brenda asked.

Ayo opened her mouth, unsure what to say, then looked over at Forrest who smiled at her, and squeezed her hand again. Was she imagining the strain around his mouth as he smiled?

"Why do we need to label everything?" Forrest said. "We enjoy being together and getting to know each other. Right, babe?"

Ayo nodded and smiled with a mirth she did not feel.

Looking down at her chicken salad, she felt instead both bile and disappointment rising simultaneously in her throat.

She was relieved she managed to excuse herself discreetly and make it to the bathroom in time. She came out from the stall and rinsed her hands and the sourness from her mouth.

Then, as she turned off the tap, she stood looking at herself in the mirror for what seemed an eternity.

Here at last was validation of her fears, of ecstasy fading, she thought bitterly as she made her way back to the table.

"Are you okay?" Forrest asked when they were back in his apartment. "You were in the restroom a long time. I missed you."

"Really?" Ayo said quietly, sullenly, as he nuzzled her neck. "Didn't seem like you needed me."

He pulled back and searched her face. "Did I do something wrong? You hardly said two words to me on the way back here."

She sighed. Perhaps she had let herself get too wrapped up in the novelty of the thing. Perhaps he was no more a sexual obsession to her than she must be to him. Perhaps what they'd had would burn itself out. But what if he thought she'd done it on purpose? How many times back home had she seen men claim women tried to "tie" them with a plate of stewed peas and rice laced with obeah spices, which led to entrapment – and more and more children?

"No. Nothing is wrong," she said. "Come 'ere."

She pulled him back into her embrace to still her own dissenting inner voice.

"Forrest?"

"Hmm?" he said, still holding her.

"*Are* we official?"

He pulled back and looked at her.

"Of course," he said, smiling. "I just didn't want them in our business. I work with them every week. They can be a little juvenile about things like this."

She looked at his dimpled smile. The answer had not been the declaration that would have buoyed her.

"And what is Brenda to you?"

She watched Forrest's face break into a grin.

"Don't tell me you're jealous," he said, shaking his head.

"I'm not," Ayo said, louder than she intended. "She's just... I know she may be better for you. I get that."

Forrest stepped back.

"What are you talking about?"

Ayo walked over to his arm chair and sank into it.

"I just wonder if we've had a moment to stop and think. You probably didn't tell them I am your girlfriend because maybe you didn't have time to think about that properly, and that is okay. You can be honest with me."

"Where is this coming from?" he said evenly, walking over to the kitchenette. Ayo watched him fill a glass with water at the sink. He gulped it down, then shook his head, chuckling.

"Don't laugh at me," Ayo said. "I'm serious."

"Maybe you just need some rest."

"Stop treating me like a child!"

Ayo found herself on her feet. She reached for her knapsack and walked briskly towards the door, but Forrest intercepted her before she got there.

"Why are you trying to pick a fight with me?" he asked, taking her face in his hands. "Why do we have to label what we are for anybody? And when have I ever treated you like a child?"

"I just don't know if I am ready for all this," Ayo said, burying her face in his shirt.

Ayo's head went back as Forrest used an index finger to prop her chin up, to make her look at him.

"You are a lovely, mature, level-headed woman," he said evenly. "And I adore you."

Ayo let him press his lips against hers, then she put her

head back against his chest. She felt him prop his chin on the crown of her head and circle his arms around her as he had done many times before. They stood like that at the doorway for a moment, breathing in tandem. This was the first time he had verbalized anything akin to love for her, but she could not understand why it did not appease her now.

"But you do treat *yourself* like a child, sometimes," he murmured, against her hair.

"Excuse me?" Ayo pulled away and stared up at him.

"Don't get mad. I mean, you let your aunt dictate who you should be. Have you told her you don't go to that Christian group on campus? Does *she* know about *me*? About *us*?"

"I have to go," Ayo said, reaching for the door knob again.

"Don't run away," he said.

"I think I may have a stomach bug."

"Don't be like that, Ayo."

"It's fine."

"Do you want me to make you some tea?"

Ayo tried not to hear the frustration in his voice. She turned and gave him a sad smile and shook her head.

"Call me when you get to that conference," she said, opening the door and slipping through it before he could object.

As she made her way to her dorm, she tried not to think about what had been forming in her mind, about what was making her ill-at-ease, despite the wonderful things he had said.

Perhaps she would not tell him at all. Perhaps she would not need to.

★

She came to the decision slowly over the week she was separated from Forrest. It became clear what she had to do when she sat at Auntie Gene's table that weekend and tried to explain why she did not want her aunt to make the saltfish fritters with the dried codfish her mother had sent along with tins of ackee and callaloo.

"Since when you don't eat good good saltfish?" her aunt asked. "And think how Charmaine mus-be save to be able to afford to send you all this."

"Maybe we can eat something American for a change, Auntie, like waffles?" Ayo said.

It was the one thing she could eat in the morning that would not hurl itself back up.

Her aunt turned and gave her a long hard look before turning back to the stove. She watched her aunt drop dollops of the saltfish batter into the oil, nausea rising.

"Hymph! If I never know better, I say is breed you breeding," Auntie Gene said flatly.

Ayo bit her lip to stop herself from the fidgeting that would surely give her away.

"But I know you are a sensible girl. Only wish you would come to prayer meeting more often," her aunt said, and Ayo felt lightheaded with relief.

"You should sing more. I tell Sister Willis you going to join the choir," her aunt continued over the crackle of the hot oil.

The early morning service at the Church of God had been a sobering reminder of what life would be like. Foot washing, head wrappings and laying on of hands. She would be tied to ritual and penance – and having a newborn to care for. She would lose more than Forrest.

She had not thought how much she would lose of herself.

"Can I call Uncle Merville?" she asked.

"Why? You have phone card?" her aunt asked.

Ayo shook her head. She had not spoken to him since she'd arrived. She wanted to speak to someone who would not require a litany of her progress. She would not have to tell him she was failing in everything but English Literature. She would not have to mention she had long lost her faith, that she might never have been truly among the converted. She would not have to ask what true love was and be told it came only from God.

She would not have to tell *him* about the baby.

"I have five minutes on this card. Why you wouldn't call your mother, child?"

Her aunt put the phone card on the table beside a plate of the hot fritters. Ayo swallowed down the dry heave.

"I talked to her last week. I just missed hearing his voice. It can wait."

Her aunt looked at her and put a hand to Ayo's forehead.

"Is okay, you can call him. I know how it is," she said.

Ayo could not prevent her eyes tearing. She hoped her aunt mistook them as mere homesickness and not the tangle of feelings she could not explain.

★

Now, as she stood there by Cypress Lake holding her stomach, Ayo felt no change. Her abdomen had contracted briefly, but she suspected that was more from hunger than from the concoction she had drunk that morning.

She touched her stomach and realized with a pang that she had never said the words, never actually uttered any declaration of love to Forrest when he told her he adored her. She did not know if she loved him. She did not know if that mattered now.

She wondered if her mother had felt this way. Had her father shrunk back with the news of her – their unexpected child? Had he already grown tired of her mother? Did he make her leave through the service gate? Had her mother, like her, felt raw inside with the fear of it? She understood, now, her mother's lifelong bid to shield her from such a fate.

When she had called him the day before from her aunt's, her uncle had sounded different, weary. Perhaps she had caught him rising from a nap, or perhaps he was unwell. She had been afraid to ask.

"That my sweet Yo-yo?" he'd said, and Ayo began to sob.

"What the matter, baby love? Everything okay with you?"

"Yes, yes," Ayo said. "I just have a cold, but I'm okay."

"So how things in big big America? Look how you turn foreigner pon we now, eh?"

"Tell me about the corn, Uncle Merville," she had said. "Tell me about the East Indian mango trees. Soon time for them, right?"

Her uncle sighed.

"We had to sell part of the land, Yo-yo, baby," her uncle said. "Times changing. Tings not so easy as one time. But when you come, there will be East Indian mango. Fat and sweet."

She had long rejected the idea of returning to Jamaica before completing her degree. How could she bring not a college degree but another mouth to feed to her mother's tenement, returning worse than she had left?

The line went dead before she could fashion a lie she could believe in – that she would instead travel back to Port Maria to the safety of Uncle Merville's farm to pretend that nothing had changed.

The line went dead before she could ask her uncle to tell her again the story of the tortoise and the porridge, how the tortoise went to an obeah man at the top of a hill to beg him to make his wife pregnant, and the obeah man made him a porridge with special roots and herbs in it. The obeah man had warned the tortoise never to let the porridge touch his tongue, and the tortoise had agreed. The journey home was long, and the porridge smelled more and more appealing. He would just look, the tortoise thought. One look led to a taste, and then halfway to his journey home, the tortoise had put the pot to his head and swallowed the whole thing. Looking down at his stomach, swollen and heavy, was the last thing he did. His poor wife found him dead days later with a child trapped in his body, with no way to get out.

As a child, Ayo had found this story as silly as any of her uncle's tales, tales meant to teach her patience and self-control. Now, they took on a menacing tone.

She looked down at the folds of her blouse. It would be a few more months before anything began to show. Then she would not be able to visit her Auntie Gene without confessing that she had arrived in January, given herself away in February, and found herself pregnant in May. She could already hear Auntie Gene's damning proclamations of her sinful nature.

Yet, even as she felt the disappointment well in the pit of her stomach that the concoction might not be working, there was something else too. Perhaps deep down, she could imagine meeting the child. She could imagine a girl, like her, whom she could teach some of what she had begun to learn about the world. They could figure it out together.

She needed to write to her mother. She did not know how she would say it, but she would assure her all was well. Then, she would have to make it so.

She looked back at the alligators swimming away from where she stood. Then she looked up at the changing sky signalling the onset of dusk.

Forrest would soon call her from the conference. There were things she wanted to say to him now.

Whatever her decision in this foreign place, it would be hers and hers alone. She slowly walked back in the direction she had come.

THE WISH

When Mama Icylda came to Beryl Hampton in the form of a river mumma, he thought his time had come. She was young-young, like those pictures he had seen of her singing and dancing in the pantomime in the forties, not the old woman who left the known world when he was a boy.

In the dream, he was at the Rio Cobre's edge, just looking into the glassy green water, blanketed by a thin mist. When it lifted, his grandmother sat on a stone, seeming to float out there like the famed golden table.

"Berry, you wasting time, mi son," she said quietly, the water taking her voice to him in waves. It was the same voice she had used to hush him to sleep when his stomach ached from eating green mango and salt when they had little else.

"You wasting time. I need you to cross this river, but I need something from you first, mi son."

At first, he did not understand her meaning. He knew that river maids and water spirits required a sacrifice of something, but he did not know what. Perhaps, he had drunk too much pomegranate wine the night before.

Yet, watching her wade toward him, it felt good to see the one good adult of his youth again, even as, at forty-six, he appeared to eclipse her by at least two decades, her taut skin making her appear as she did in her twenties, her wild hair piled high with a strange array of Spanish needle and cerasee bush, as though they were the very crown jewels. He couldn't see clearly if her fingers were webbed or if she still had the varicose veins he used to trace up and down her limbs.

"What you mean, Mama?"

When she reached to touch his face, he awoke with the words still on his lips.

★

He was still pondering the dream when he went to the supermarket to get a custard cake for his birthday. As he left the mart, he retrieved the handbill the supermarket bagger had stuffed in his scandal bag.

The neon orange flyer had a message in bold, black font. At first, it made his chest tighten in fear, as all words did, but he made himself decipher the letters.

"Do ... you ... want ... to ... be ... a ... star?"

He looked at the image of the man with a microphone and the Island Records logo he had seen many times on local television, and recognized that this was an advert for the annual singing contest. He studied the picture of the man posed with his eyes closed, one hand extended, and his mouth wide, as though belting out a sustained note.

It dawned on him what he must do.

What did it matter that he had never sung a note in public before? The conviction swelled across his chest.

It felt like an omen that on his birthday he should receive a handbill with words he could actually read, words that signalled his looming stardom the day after his grandmother had seen fit to cross the bridge between his world and hers to tell him he had to act.

★

Back home, he looked at the flyer again. It stood out in the sparse room, part kitchenette, dining, and living room, with a brown sofa facing the 14-inch television. The only other bright spot was a vase of bougainvillea he had placed on the table that day, flowers he'd cut from the neighbour's plant hanging into his yard.

He shifted in the wooden chair that squeaked under his weight, thinking grimly he had reached the age when his father had died of cirrhosis of the liver.

He had accomplished little in his life. Each year, he had watched as tweens, teenagers, and twenty-somethings paraded across his television screen vying for a singing contract with Island Records and the fifty-thousand-dollar cash prize.

He was twenty-eight when the contest began and he'd been on the fringes of the crowd of would-bes and hope-fors in Parade Square. Back then, it had never occurred to him to go up with those in line to be considered. He had watched the auditions for a moment, then turned and walked home.

Music had been a part of his youth – as sound systems playing in the distance on Sundays, as a soundtrack to the neighbour cutting the grass in his yard, the housewife hanging white bush jackets on wires propped up by bamboo stalks, or for the boys playing football in the lane. Music was for everyone to enjoy, but not something for him to pursue.

In primary school days, sprawled underneath the little brick house, he'd listen to his father's Peter Tosh and Barrington Levy tapes on an old cassette player – while he should have been completing his lessons.

Once, two boys heard him bellowing the words to "Mystic Man". They had come into the yard to find Beryl there on his back, warbling.

"You sound like some donkey dem-a torture over de slaughterhouse," one of them said.

"No, like when some cat inna heat," the other said, and slapped his friend's shoulder.

After Beryl chased them away, he went back to listening

to his tapes, shaking off the dejection their mockery had made him feel.

Now he was older and wiser. He could not let a little thing such as having no experience deter his ambitions. What did it matter that he was twice or even three times the average contestant's age?

It was *his* time now.

★

The room felt even smaller when Eden arrived, the twenty-something cashier from the Island Grill with whom he'd begun a dalliance over the past two months. He smiled at her round, young face, beaming in that way she had when she was pleased with her own joke. She had squeezed forty-six candles onto the misshapen coconut custard cake, announcing that this celebrated Beryl's steady approach to a half a century of life.

"I did think you would need my help blowing out all them candles," Eden chuckled.

"One candle would-a be enough. Is a safety hazard you causing just to make fun that I getting old?" Beryl shook his head as she removed the candles and cut a wedge of cake for him.

"Never mind. You are *my* old man," she said as she handed him the slice. He felt her lips kissing the bald spot at the top of his head.

Eden had also decorated the cake with his name in small loops of sugar-free icing. The "y" from "birthday" was still attached to his slice. When he was six, Mama Icylda had sat with him out in her backyard in Eltham Acres under the tamarind tree and taught him how to write the five letters of his name. It took her weeks and weeks. Other children called him a duncebat; she had called him her "bright little Berry" and patted his head for every effort. He remembered her bony fingers, her warm, cloudy eyes, and the coconut drops she made when he could finally do it. This was long after other children his age were reading about white children like Dick, Jane, and their dog named Spot, or the stories about Boysie and Anancy in the local readers the Ministry of Education were bringing in.

"You too sof' wid him, Mama," he remembered his father saying in one of his rare lucid moments. "The boy need a firm hand. Him not paying attention when he at school. That is him problem."

"But him need the help, Desmond," she had said. "Him need plenty help. He just don't see or understand things like you and me. I been trying to find out what really wrong."

Perhaps if she had lived to see him turn seven, Beryl would not have spent the next four decades unable to read much else, managing to get by only by knowing common one or two syllable words whipped into him by the woman his father married when Mama Icylda died – his step-mother, Eve.

It was Eve's constant scowling that made her fearsome, made her limbs seem long and menacing, despite her short stature. She would strike him for every mistake. This began the day when he brought back the wrong brand of cigarettes.

"You don't know this?" She held up the Craven 'A' carton. "The next time you don't bring no Matterhorn, I beat you until you soft."

"Look at me!" she demanded and grabbed the grade three reader from his hands and flipped through the pages.

"Read me something!" When Beryl stumbled, he got a stroke for every word he missed. That day he learned "bat" and "boy" and "look" and "give" and "mango", each with blows. As an adult he spent years relying on his memory. He knew it would have saddened his grandmother.

It was music that made him feel better inside. Once, he burrowed a hole in the back yard and crawled in it, partly to escape one of his stepmother's whippings while his father lay drunk and oblivious, and partly so he could listen to the neighbour playing the Mighty Diamonds' album, *Right Time*.

At sixteen he ran away. Then he could play Yellow Man and Gregory Isaacs and listen in the solitude of a tiny little back room and quietly sing along.

He had left high school at sixteen with just a school leaving certificate, but then had learned one skill that served him well for a time – the art of topiary.

He was out delivering oranges – the only job he could get without having to fill in a form – when he saw a man shearing the hedges in a stately uptown yard on the better side of Kingston. He watched the man for hours as he transformed the bush into a pig shape. He noticed, too, the row of human forms in the background – lingering on one section that looked like floating breasts – for which Beryl later learned the client's neighbour had reported him to the police.

Intrigued, Beryl started shouting questions to the man, eventually asking if he'd be willing to train him.

"Why I mus do that for a street boy like you?" The man regarded Beryl with a look that made him feel every bit a pauper, standing beside his handcart in his faded T-shirt and threadbare jeans.

"I is not a street boy, sah. I was saying if I could do half as good as you, sah, be like your assistant or something, I could make myself useful for once."

He had wanted to curse the man for putting him down, but tightened his hands on the steering wheel of his cart to restrain himself. He had long learned that honey worked better than a mouth full of vinegar on most everyone.

He had lived on his own from the age of sixteen in a

church lady's back room. He had never become one of the boys harassing motorists at stoplights with their squeegees and buckets of dirty soapy water to smear across windshields for spare change.

Perhaps it was the promise of free labour that made the man, Ezra Cunningham, change his mind. They agreed on a six-week unpaid apprenticeship, and it was as if Beryl had been born with a pair of shears in his hands, exhibiting what Cunningham said was the eye of a true artisan. One time they went to work at Devon House and there were always admiring audiences watching him and Cunningham transform the dense foliage into flamingos, peacocks, and miniature elephants with tusks to scale.

It did not take long for Cunningham to realize that Beryl could only decode information through things like logos or accompanying pictures, and not by reading the actual words, save for the few he had learnt like hieroglyphics, courtesy of Eve.

For a time, Beryl did not realize how much of his wages Cunningham was syphoning off – not until the church lady who had given him the room – and had become more lover than landlady – asked him why his pay was getting less and less each month.

"Is just that tax gone up," Beryl said. "He show me some papers and things and say it was just inflation and how it does affect everyone pay."

"Nobody cannot be so damn fool," the woman said, and tossed his tool bag and sparse clothing out onto the steps.

Beryl did not keep women for long, and many he was not sad to see go, but this had been a harsh lesson. He had to find another warm bed and make his way again.

He attracted women with his vigorous lovemaking, but they would only endure his simple ways for a time. It would take them about two months to figure out his illiteracy, and then he would hear them ask loudly why they had bothered to be around such a simpleton. His excuses of weak eyesight, blurry vision, and migraines only worked for a while.

But now there was Eden and they would see.

★

The day he met her had not been particularly remarkable. He had walked into the Island Grill off Half Way Tree Road during their busy Wednesday lunch hour and pointed to the picture of fricassee chicken and seasoned fries. She had rung up his order with no sign she had noticed him. He noted the dimpled smile she gave customers, the way she held herself erect, the way she hummed while she made change and sang along to the Tanya Stephens ballad blaring in the restaurant. Her voice was sweet.

"You should be the one singing on the radio," Beryl said, getting up with his tray, when he had finished eating and the crowd had thinned.

"What?" She glanced over at him, then back at the coins she was counting.

"I say you should be singing for real, like on the radio." She huffed.

"No. I serious. Where you learn to sing like that?"

"I used to sing in church when I was little." Her dimples flashed at him.

Before he could continue, a man with a headset walked up to them from the rear of the kitchen, saying, "Eden, we need someone to go clean up the grease on the grill."

"You buying something else, sah?" he asked Beryl, and something in his tone made Beryl agitated, as though his patronizing the establishment meant nothing.

But he only shook his head and walked away to wait for an hour or two for Eden to emerge at the end of her shift.

"You know I should call police and say this strong-back man out here lay-waiting me," Eden said with a good-natured smile. Without her apron, he saw she wore a blouse and jeans pants that hugged her like a second skin.

"Couldn't let a pretty little song bird like you fly away," he said, pleased he had managed to say the line he had been rehearsing.

She had looked him over, and his confidence ebbed as he imagined how he must appear to her with his thinning hair, stocky build, and bushy eyebrows, and yet her smile appeared to mean she liked what she saw.

"Buy me a drink over at Red Bones and maybe I sing you a song," she said.

★

Now, Eden was looking over his shoulder at the flyer.

"Is what this?" Her bosom pressed against his back and he thought of the special lovemaking she had promised to give him that night.

"Is the singing contest," Beryl said, taking another bite of cake and wishing he could enjoy real sugar and not this pasty substitute Eden had insisted he buy to safeguard against diabetes. He knew it only because of its red packaging; she had bought it before.

"You know, maybe… maybe the both of we can enter together," he began tentatively, using the fork to crush the rest of the cake and not looking back at her right away.

"What you talking about, *me* and *you*?"

She took up the flyer. Beryl did not like the way her incredulity hung in the silence.

"Regular somebody like you and me don't stand no chance," she said. "Everybody know is biased these contests biased. Look how last year, the singer that win is only because she did know the judge family member personal."

"This year is *my* time though," Beryl said, but the words sounded strange outside his head. He thought again of his grandmother's words, *You wasting time, mi son,* and the warm feeling that flooded through him when he first read the flyer. How could he let go of it now?

"This is *my* time," he said, this time more to himself.

Eden looked back at him. This time, he did not find her dimpling cheeks endearing. He did not find it amusing that her whole frame trembled with suppressed laughter.

"Berry, stop talking nonsense. I don't even hear you sing in the bathroom. Where you get this idea?" Her laughter escaped in ripples until her large bosom shook.

"You know what? We could…" She caught her breath between laughs. "We could … go old school like those songs you always playing. I'd be J. C. Lodge and you'd be Shabba, right? We could sing 'Telephone Love' for the judges, don't?"

It would have bothered him less that she laughed if he hadn't already begun to visualize himself on stage, that people would look at him with admiration as they had done in his youth when he was creating his green sculptures. He had even been in *The Gleaner* once.

But after Cunningham sacked him when he confronted him about the money, going solo didn't work out. His respectable clients refused to pay him cash, finding it odd that Beryl did not wish to sign contracts or accept cheques. Then, even the much smaller clientele, who didn't mind paying cash, began to fall off; times were hard and creating fancy shapes from bushes was too damn frivolous. By then the joy had gone out of the little work he could get.

Over the last few months, Eden had sated his disappointments and sorrows in the warmth of her body, but now her giggling grated on his nerves. He had never felt so old; she could not recognize how much he had needed this one possibility.

"Well, Berry, at least there's no age restrictions," she was saying now, winded from laughing, using a paper napkin to dab away tears. "So, I mus call you Beres Hammond now? You have the same initials and everything. Sing something for me, nuh Beres?"

He let her laugh her fill and when she was quiet, he took up his plate and went to the sink, ignoring her, letting the water run and pulse through the room.

"You not angry?" she had said, sobering only for a moment, her laughter still there like a percolating coffeepot on a lowered flame. "You was serious, Berry?"

Beryl sighed.

"It was just a stupid likkle thought," he murmured, picking up the sponge to wash the plate.

How easily she had done it. The idea had lived and died in one afternoon and now he could see the stupidity of it. The old, festering self-loathing returned. He moved the sponge around and around, watching the remnants of the cake wash down the drain, feeling a familiar heaviness settle on his chest.

He tried to remember what his grandmother had looked like in the dream and failed. More vivid was the memory of her lying cold in the house, her head wrapped in white, her hands folded across her white dress in the cedar coffin while Beryl's father sang sankey after sankey, aided by white rum and grief. The spectacle had felt raw – the contrast between the repose of her body and people gyrating as though they were at a dance and not a dead yard. Perhaps that was why she had come to him, because she was not at peace.

He listened to Eden singing a few bars of Beres

Hammond's "Can You Play Some More". He knew it was to mock him and felt a pulsing at his temples.

A terrible thought flittered through his mind. What would it be like to wrap his soapy hands around her neck until she stopped laughing? He would look down on her silent and still and perhaps he would be the one to sing a sankey for her so her spirit could travel away from him in peace at her own wake.

"But Berry, you never read the whole of it?" she asked, holding out the flyer. "Them say no duets, groups, or bands, and plus, you never see the date already pass for the Kingston auditions. The next place is all the way in MoBay."

Beryl turned off the tap and turned to look at her. All of the excuses were ready in his mind to reel off quickfire.

"I can't read it," he said instead, surprised at how easily the words came out of him. Perhaps they had come that way because, just then, he wanted her to go and take away her laughter. But when she stood looking at him, all traces of mirth gone from her face, he regretted his bald honesty.

"I was wondering about that," she said quietly.

He hated the silence that hovered like a palpable thing.

"I can help you if you want," she said finally.

He did not look at her right away, blinking back tears.

"But Berry, if anyone is entering that contest, is me, because we both know you not a singer," she said, coming to wrap her arms around his thickening waist.

He stood still for a beat longer, letting her embrace him.

"Maybe you can help me wid that too," he said.

"One thing at a time," she said. "I never say I can promise miracles."

This time when he felt the vibrations of her laughter, he let it infect him, dissolving something hard in his chest.

WALKER WOMAN

Sophia sat on her ledge counting the times the old woman walked the path through the apartment courtyard. The tally was seventeen times in fifty-eight minutes.

The first time she noticed the woman was two months before, when she had just arrived. As she'd made her second trip from her car up to the apartment, she'd stopped on the stairs, holding the last suitcase, and watched the woman walk by her for a third time.

In the weeks that followed, the counting game became a means to stave off boredom. How many times a day did the old woman do this? How many times had she donned that hunter-green velvet track suit and walked the path across the parking lot, through the breezeway to the fountain, then back to the parking lot from the opposite side?

Now, as she sat by the window to let out the cigarette smoke and coax in the grudging summer breeze, Sophia saw once again the familiar green track suit, the thinning salt and pepper bob, the gauntness and blotchy pink skin, and the cigarette butt the woman would periodically purse to her lips as she walked.

Why this incessant walking? Here comes another cycle – number eighteen. Perhaps walking could cure homesickness too. Maybe she should join the woman on the nineteenth loop.

After twenty times, Sophia got up. Sunday afternoon had to be saved from being completely unproductive.

As she walked by her housemate's bedroom, she re-

flected how little she'd engaged with Elaine. She was fre-
quently away, travelling for work as an air-hostess, but they
had little to say when she was there. Was this because Elaine
was the first white person she had ever lived with?

Better at least than her previous roommate in Havendale
– a fifty-year-old East Indian man who'd taken to walking
pants-less across their shared passageway. She had only
endured his increasingly odd behaviour because she knew
she would soon be going away to graduate school in Georgia, taking her away from the desolation that had been her
life for the past two years.

She went to water Elaine's drooping ivories on the
kitchen window sill. She looked down and saw the woman
had stopped walking and was staring up at her. She moved
out of view and for a few beats stood shielded behind the
chiffon curtains before peeking out again to find the woman
was gone. Maybe she was like those shape-shifting crea-
tures of her father's stories – like the woman who could step
out of her skin and become a gazelle, or who could disappear in a wink and sink to the bottom of the Rio Cobre.

What made her so uneasy about this woman? Her slow
gait, or her sunken blank stare? She had spoken to her just
three times since moving in. She'd been putting coins in the
dryer, when the woman suddenly appeared beside her and
murmured, "Machine works now, huh?"

"Yes. Seems so," she'd said, grabbing her basket, and half
walked, half ran back upstairs to the haven of her unit.

Another time, she'd gone out on the balcony for her
morning smoke and found the woman looking up at her.

"You got up early, huh?" the woman said.

"Yes. I did," she'd said, crushing the half-smoked butt
and quickly retreating inside. Later she'd wondered if the
velvet track suit was one of many or the same one recycled.

The last time was when she was rushing out to the parking lot and nearly collided with the woman.

"Late for work, huh?"

"Yes. I am," she'd said, and quickly got into her second-hand Volkswagen bug and driven away.

She hadn't expected the adjustment to this place to be this difficult. It often felt surreal with this wandering old woman and the absentee roommate. Added to the mix was the silent blond man and his three-legged dog next door, the Indian nurse and the black policeman. They seemed like an offbeat troupe of circus performers who did not speak to each other, though thrust together in these grey-stone apartments.

The silence was still strange. Before Havendale with its disrobing landlord, she had lived on a lane in rural Saint Thomas where she knew the names of every child, every old man, every baby mother and every constable. If you passed an adult without saying "Good Morning", "Good Afternoon" or "Good Evening", loud and clear, it was seen as rude. Only when she'd moved to the heart of Kingston had she experienced the silence of strangers in public places.

★

It was a particularly warm day when Sophia saw the "Walker Woman", wearing galoshes and walking a bulldog. She wore the bottom half of the velvet track suit and a white blouse more suited to the intense heat.

Sophia did not realize how long she'd been staring until the walker woman tried to wave and her dog leapt into her arms, knocking her over. Despite her fear of dogs, she sprinted over and pulled the woman to her feet.

"Sinclair, behave," the woman grumbled as the dog yipped at Sophia's legs.

"You alright, ma'am?" Sophia asked, casting a wary eye at the growling dog.

"I'm okay now. Thank you, dear," the woman said in what Sophia thought was a thick Southern drawl. She had reclaimed the leash and pulled the dog toward her.

Sophia looked down at the woman's galoshes and then quizzically up at the expanse of blue sky, not one rain cloud in sight. Here was an opportunity to ask about the incessant walking and the strange uniform, but it seemed odd to just ask her outright.

"Where you get those galoshes?" she heard herself ask instead. "They're very stylish."

The woman looked down on the mustard yellow boots with a smile.

"At the flea market, dear. They have all kinds of interesting things. I used to go every week, but it's too much these days."

"Oh," Sophia said, not sure what else to say. She watched the walker woman hold her hip as she tried to take a step.

"You need some help?"

The woman held out her arm in reply, and Sophia took it.

"Come, Sinclair," the walker woman said to the dog.

Close to her, Sophia could smell a strange odour of camphor balls and rubbing alcohol. It reminded her of her own maternal grandmother from St. Thomas, though Granny Ivy smelled like primroses and white rum.

"Where are you from, dear?" the woman asked.

"Jamaica," Sophia said, scolding herself quietly for having feared the woman. She could feel how frail she was through the material of the blouse.

"Oh, I know all about Jamaica," she said. "I have a few books about the Caribbean."

Sophia hoped they would get to the door before the

woman continued this line of talk. She hated to field questions about Jamaica's square footage, population, and national language – sure she would be asked something she ought to know but did not.

Luckily, the woman asked no more, and said, "I can make it from here."

Sophia still held the arm, uncertain.

Perhaps if she had been prepared for it, Sophia would not have stood open-mouthed as the woman opened her door. She would have found something clever to say to bide her time, so she could take in what she was seeing.

The opened door revealed old newspapers, yellowing books, heaps of clothes everywhere, half-open and rusting tins of canned food piled so high they made peaks that pressed against the ceiling. Sophia spotted a small path in the valley between the mounds of food wrappers and balled-up paper towels before the woman slipped inside, pulling the bull dog behind her and shutting the door without a word of thanks or goodbye.

Sophia stood there for moment longer before making her way to the other side of the complex, worry and pity merging.

★

She had not seen the walker woman for three days, nor the dog. Each morning she opened the window to let out the cigarette smoke and waited, but there were no sightings.

When Elaine came back for a couple of days, Sophia broke their unwritten code and asked, "Um, you know the walker woman that lives downstairs?"

"The what?"

"Oh, sorry," Sophia said, chuckling. "I mean, the old lady who walks around the parking lot all the time. You know anything about her?"

Sophia stood there feeling awkward as Elaine watched the plate go around and around in the microwave in their shared kitchen.

"You know, I don't think I got her name, and I've lived here for five years," she said. "Why do you ask?"

"Just curious. I haven't seen her in a while. Do you know why she does that? Just walking and walking. She crazy?"

"Don't know. I guess I never thought about it."

The microwave dinged, and Elaine smiled at her in that strained way of many Americans. She found herself doing it too, to her classmates and professors, making a smile that was just spreading the corners of her lips across, instead of upwards.

Despite her hopes for a roommate who left her to her own devices and never peppered her with questions about her past, she was beginning to resent Elaine's reticence. There were no great secrets to be exposed. She'd had little in the way of a love life, had gone through her teenage years with both parents alive and well, had never had a run-in with school administration or law enforcement. There had been Roger, but she didn't want to think about him – but the general loneliness that existed as a hum most of her life had amplified to a shrill. Could it be curbed with even a cursory interest from this new roommate? She wanted to ask her about her job, about whether she flew international, about stories of rude passengers, or celebrity interactions, or near-death experiences.

Once, Elaine had knocked on her door to offer her pizza, but her dairy intolerance meant she had to decline.

"Oh, thanks for trying to revive my plants," Elaine said, almost at the doorway. "I've tried a self-watering system, but they're a lost cause."

Sophia attended to the plants every day when she came in

from school. She had even bought a croton to keep the ivories company; her father said plants were sociable organisms. She'd gotten them plant food and taken them out on the patio so they could get more sun in the mornings, but she had begun to lose hope. At home, ivories were easy, low-maintenance plants. Her mother had them coiling up the grillwork on the front porch back in St. Thomas, but here Elaine's ivories just would not thrive. Yet the more they defied help, the more Sophia yearned to help them. It became as much an obsession as spying on the old woman.

She'd never been one to insert herself in the affairs of others. *Cockroach no business in a fowl fight,* as Jamaicans said. It had kept her safe when classmates squabbled over sports or love interests. She had known to stay at her desk against the wall when one classmate called another "hairy-hairy like dog" and leapt at the girl, screaming that she better leave her boyfriend alone because her man did not sleep with animals.

Sophia was never among the children wrestling out there on the savannah, or having sex in the bathroom, or hiding on the train line learning to roll a proper spliff. She had kept only three friends from primary school through high school. The one who'd worked with her at her old job had not even wished her happy trails when she learnt of Sophia's impending migration.

Her mother called her a good-good girl because she never missed a Sunday call home, not even when she moved to Kingston out of their sight, and stopped attending church, or here in Georgia. She spoke to her parents just before their morning prayers at eight o'clock every Sunday, or before they went out to service at four in the afternoon. They could not dream she spoke to them through puffs of smoke, her one vice, picked up from her ex-boyfriend – the only thing he gave her willingly – that and an unwrapped umbrella he gave her for Valentine's Day. Even so, they would never have to worry about her going to rum bars or dance halls or dens of iniquity, as her grandmother called any place that did not require a head covering and a New Testament bible.

So she was not going to lose sleep over why Elaine was so distant or whether the old woman might or might not be dead under her rubbish hoard, her corpse devoured by a bulldog called Sinclair.

*

Two days passed before she saw the walker woman again. Elaine had left for work, and Sophia decided to go out on the patio to try again with the ivories.

The walker woman was back in her velvet sweat suit, standing over the small pot beside the crotons that Sophia used as a makeshift ashtray. She watched the woman fish out a soggy butt and bring it to her lips.

"Hey, wait!"

"Oh!" The old woman jumped and dropped the butt.

Sophia pulled a carton from her pocket and offered the woman a cigarette. She had seen the woman do this before, looking in little pots or cups left beside the patio furniture, but not knowing she was searching for castaways.

"They say these will kill you," Sophia said, chuckling lightly as she offered the woman a light.

"Well, I've been smoking since 1958 and I'm not dead yet," the woman said.

"Everything okay? Where's the dog?" Sophia asked. This close to her, the woman's weathered face seemed almost familiar.

"My son came for Sinclair," she said, puffing. "He said I can't take care of him, but I would've liked to have spent one more afternoon with him."

"Why you can't see him again? You can't go visit him sometime?" Sophia asked.

The woman puffed in silence.

"I guess I forget sometimes," she said. "My son says I need supervision now."

"You like to walk a lot," Sophia began tentatively.

"Oh, yes," the woman said. "Exercise keeps me young."

"You seem to walk the same path every day. It don't get a little too much fo' you?" Sophia sat on the edge of the railing, facing the woman, looking at her cloudy grey eyes.

There was something in the woman's stare that seemed less vacant today.

"It's what Eustace likes," she said casually.

"Eustace?"

"My husband of sixty-four years. We walk together every day. We used to live on a farm in Slidell, Louisiana. You know it?"

Sophia shook her head.

"He would make his morning rounds every day, so we continue to do it here. I can't let him do it by himself."

"We?"

"Yes, we still make our morning rounds and our evening rounds here. It's just a little different here is all. No cattails or marshland or cypress trees."

Or Eustace, Sophia added to herself.

She followed the woman's gaze across the pool to her apartment door. What must it be like to live like that, to bury oneself in things? Perhaps Eustace was a figment of her mind, or perhaps the loss of him had taken away her mind. Sophia could never imagine loving anyone so much.

When she'd met Roger, it had been casual from the beginning. He was someone to fill in the moments between inputting numbers in spreadsheets at work and lying in her narrow bed at night. They'd met at a bus stop and he'd shared his giant blue-striped umbrella when the rain came in through the roof with holes like a sieve. Then they'd gone to an Island Grill and talked over a yabba bowl of fricassee chicken. Two weeks later, they lay in her twin-sized bed chatting after sex, a couple of Craven A's, and the TVJ news.

At times she'd relished when he was gone. She never pined for him, though she wasn't totally without feeling for him. She did like his broad shoulders and dimpled chin. She softened at the boy-like joy he took in any physical humour and trying to make her laugh. Yet she often felt fatigued by his presence and sometimes blew off long standing engagements with him just for a quiet evening of tea and TV.

He wanted to marry her after the first month. She had said no. After two years, he asked her again, and she again refused. Then, he went to Fort Clarence and drowned.

Just like that, he was gone.

Sophia had realized then how little she really needed and how much he had become a part of her small piece of happiness.

"So, how did you meet Eustace?" she asked.

"When he was in short pants," the old woman said. "He stole my pencil and wouldn't give it back. I told the teacher and she put us on the same bench because she said we needed to learn to get on."

"So how you know you wanted to be with him? To be his wife?"

The walker woman was silent for a moment, pulling on the cigarette and watching the cloud of smoke as she exhaled.

"He left for the war when I was just sixteen. He was gone so long, I was just a girl when he left. I didn't want to get married when he came back. I wanted to go away to college

first, even though my mama said I needed to get on up out
her house. I was still so young, you see."

She fell silent again.

"Where are you from, dear?" she asked.

Sophia looked at her for a moment. The walker woman
showed no signs of confusion or jest.

"Jamaica."

"Oh, I know all about Jamaica," she said. "I have books on
the Caribbean."

"Yes. Yes, I know." Sophia said quietly.

Then she watched the woman drop the butt in the
makeshift tray and without a word of thanks or goodbye,
walk away toward the staircase.

★

Sophia had just pulled into the parking lot when she saw a
man standing there beside a pick-up truck with the walker
woman. Could she have been wrong? Was this Eustace?
Could she have managed to miss all the times Eustace
walked with her as the woman had claimed? But when she
looked again, she saw that the man was holding a clipboard
and could not be older than forty-five.

The walker woman seemed more agitated than usual,
pacing back and forth as a younger man got out of the pick-
up and came toward her. He had the same angular gauntness as the woman; Sophia surmised that this must be the
son who had taken Sinclair from her.

"There is no other way," the young man was saying. "You
can't continue to live like this. What if you slip and fall and
there's no one around to help you, Mama."

"I've been taking care of myself for all these years," she
said. "I took care of you and your brother real good, or don't
you remember?"

Sophia watched the young man put a hand to his brow.

"Give me the key, Mama," he said.

"If you want to get inside to touch my things, then you have to open the door your own goddamn self. I have things to do! Oh, and there is my friend," she said.

Sophia realized the woman was talking about her. Before she could move, the walker woman made a slow trek over to her.

They go need a massive truck, an eighteen-wheeler, to remove all her shit, Sophia thought absently, and smiled despite herself as the woman approached.

"You have any cigarettes?"

Sophia felt in her pocket for the carton, opening it to find a solitary cigarette.

"I only have the one." She had been saving it.

"That's okay, dear," the walker woman said, reaching for the cigarette, then motioning for a light.

"I was going to quit today anyway." Sophia flicked the lighter to flame.

"I don't know why he doesn't stay in his own house and leave me in peace," the woman said after a puff of smoke.

"Who are those people?" Sophia asked.

"I don't have a clue. They want to take me to a home and go through my things. That's all I know. They have no right!"

Sophia regarded her for a moment, wondering if she had the right to ask any questions or even offer any suggestions. She had never seen the woman so incensed.

"Perhaps, you could let them take away only the things you don't need," she offered. *Like maybe all your roach-infested shit.*

"I need ALL of it!" the walker woman snapped. "And besides, Eustace would not want me to part with any of his things."

So, she did understand. Perhaps she did know that Eustace was gone.

"He wouldn't?" Sophia was not quite sure what else to say.

"He would not."

Sophia made her way up the stairs.

"You think I belong in a home?" the walker woman asked.

"I think you should do what is right for you," Sophia said over her shoulder, getting into her apartment before the woman could question her some more.

Why did she attract such odd people? A girl in her calculus class had come up to her as everyone spilled out of the lecture room, a girl with bleached-blonde hair and a nose ring. She'd asked if she knew a Timothy from St. Ann's Bay. Sophia thought the girl's ring, looping through both nostrils, made her look like the fabled rolling calf.

She had almost said, Yes. I know every obscure person of the 2.5 million population in Jamaica and, more pointedly, your Timothy No Last Name from a large bay area in the parish of St. Ann.

"We're small. Just not that small," she said instead, with a good-natured smile.

"Oh, I guess it's crazy to think you would, just like that," the girl said. "It's just when you spoke in class today, you reminded me of him."

Sophia softened a little; the honeyed way the girl had spoken made her think that perhaps this Timothy was more than someone she'd just seen, perhaps some love interest past or current or hoped for.

But the furthest she had ventured with her class mates was to go with a few of them for coffee at one of the campus cafes. She had been surprised when she had not felt alien as they talked about the difficulty of the class, their majors, and the burden of their giant student loan debts.

Now, she felt isolated as she entered the empty apartment. Sometimes she went out to the park to watch egrets and ducks and people, but it only reminded her of home. Strangely, she had never felt connected to the land her parents' house and farm sat on, until she was here, three thousand miles away, looking at poultry and greenery in another man's country.

She looked over the parking lot to see the walker woman standing with the manager of the apartment complex. She had rarely seen this woman – a round brunette with a pleasant dimpling smile – other than behind the desk in her office, and that sole time when she had shown Sophia the apartment. Here she was talking with her hands, trying to pacify the walker woman by rubbing her shoulders. Then, they both began walking towards the courtyard.

She wanted to see the manager's face at the discovery of the monstrous hoard, but then it occurred to her that she must have known. There had been inspections: uniformed men had come to see her apartment with cameras and had evidently taken pictures.

The manager, the son, and the man with the clipboard came across the courtyard with the walker woman straggling behind. Something in the way they all paused at the door made Sophia realize that while none showed surprise when the door was opened, they were as struck with the sheer magnitude of it all as she had been.

Sophia watched the walker woman turn and walk away as the others climbed into the giant rat's nest. She did not look up as she walked by. She felt sad for the strange woman.

★

This was to be her first experience with a tornado, not

counting the one she witnessed in *The Wizard of Oz* as a child on syndicated TV back home. There was nothing sepia about this coming tornado, the weatherman was saying, showing swirls of red and yellow over the green maps, in the way that meteorologists back home showed the eye of a category five hurricane that would devastate the island.

Sophia sat watching television, wondering if Elaine was flying away or into this disaster and wondering what she would say to her if she came back to find the apartments in fragments.

How could she prepare? They had no basement. Was it masking tape or duct tape that one used on windows? Would she have to crouch down under a table or was that with earthquakes?

She looked outside to see it was already raining. The clouds were deep grey and ominous, but there was no whirling vortex coming towards them. She saw the policeman putting a board over his windows and the blond man shuffling across from the laundry room with a bag of clothes. The nurse's car was not in her parking spot. Perhaps she had decided to stay at the hospital.

Then she saw the walker woman appear, without umbrella, without rain jacket, and even her mustard yellow galoshes. No velvet track suit. She wore a mid-calf, paisley summer dress, a white cardigan, and white sneakers. Her wispy hair had been curled and she wore glasses with the chain still attached. She was almost unrecognizable.

Four months had passed since the manager, the walker woman's son, and the man with the clipboard had stepped into the hoard. What a spectacle it had been. People from the apartment complex across the road had come to see the things that were being taken out of the woman's home.

Even a camera crew had come, sent for by the son, some said. It took them a week to clear the apartment. They counted four cat carcasses and countless rodent remains. There were dirty clothes still with the tags intact, and Tupperware with shrink wrap still in place alongside the mouldy fruit and used adult diapers. The woman had wailed and wailed. Sophia did not want to see the woman's anguish, and tried hard not to listen.

As each day passed, it had become less strange not to see the walker woman making her way across the parking lot, through the breezeway to the fountain and back from the other side.

Now, there she stood as always.

Sophia hesitated, then, cursing herself, pushed her feet into her slippers, grabbed her umbrella and raced out to the parking lot.

"Hey!" she called.

The walker woman continued along the pathway.

"Hey!" Sophia called again.

This time she stopped and looked back at Sophia.

"Tornado coming. It's not safe," Sophia said, sheltering them both with the large striped umbrella. "How you get here?"

"I walked."

"From where?"

The nearest nursing home was at least five miles away. Sophia had seen it near the Goodwill on her way to school, but was that where the walker woman had been sent?

"From that place my son put me in. I'm not going back there. Eustace isn't there."

Sophia sighed. The rain had lessened, but the trees were swaying – like when hurricanes sliced through her island.

"You can't stay here. You'll get hurt."

"I don't care," the woman grumbled. "We have to keep walking."

Sophia resisted the urge to shake the woman, to grab her by the hand, and haul her inside. Why was she still involving herself in this woman's life? How had this become her problem? She could walk away and leave her out there, but something in the woman's struggle had touched her.

"He's gone!" Sophia shouted, almost involuntarily.

The woman stopped but did not turn around.

"*You* are still here. You have to keep living, lady. He is the one that is dead! You're still here. He's gone," she said again, more quietly, more to herself.

The walker woman stood close to Sophia, the rain starting up again more ardently.

"I know it must feel like a giant hole in your life, but people pass on... and your Eustace... he's dead, ma'am."

"Not to me, dear," the walker woman said. "Not to me."

Sophia bowed her head and sniffled. Then, raising her eyes again, she said, "At least take this." She extended the umbrella to the woman.

Again, without a word of thanks or goodbye, the woman ambled away.

Sophia walked back to her apartment, thinking she must call someone, though she still did not know the woman's name. The police would ask her which nursing home, and she would not be able to tell them. What could she say? There was a strange old woman walking out to meet the tornado?

Sophia went back up to her window and looked out at the woman making winding circles in the rain. Despite it all, there was something comforting about watching her. Then, just as Sophia was about to move away, the woman stopped and looked up at her as she had done that first day. Her short hair had lost its curls and was clinging to her skull. This time, Sophia did not hide behind the curtain. This time, she gave the woman a smile.

Perhaps the tornado would not come; many hurricanes had veered away from her island at the last minute before their threatened landfall.

★

This tornado did come, but five miles away from where her apartment was. The next morning she sat watching the televised images of rubble left in its wake – cars picked up and thrust nose first into the swollen rivers and mud, houses like matchsticks shredded to bits.

She went out to see if the woman was there. She found only the striped umbrella in the fountain and picked it out. How had she let herself succumb to feelings she thought dormant or nonexistent?

She hoped she would never find out what happened to the walker woman. She would not let herself believe the woman would be found drowned in a muddy ravine somewhere, as she had seen on the television that morning. She would let herself believe the old woman had simply found another parking lot to pace, somewhere else to exorcise her loss. She shook the excess water from the umbrella, rolled it up, and walked inside.

HELP WANTED

The woman was late! Forty-five minutes late. That damn security officer was looking me up and down as he passed by. Being in the US without papers is no joke. Always I have to make myself invisible.

I slipped two quarters into the payphone and dialled the woman's number.

"Hello?"

"Hello, ma'am? Is Delvina, ma'am. Is where you are, ma'am? I been waiting for quite a while now."

"How is it you don't have a cellphone in this day and age? I've been at the station for at least an hour."

"But I've been here at Grand Central, just as you say, ma'am."

The woman exhaled slowly.

"Delvina, we live in New Jersey, so why d'you go all the way to New York? You need to get back on the train and stop off at New Jersey. *New. Jersey*. Do you understand?"

Raas. She mus think me is a real idiot. I wanted to snatch the phone off the wall but carefully put it back on its hook as the security officer passed again. I sat back down to wait on the next train.

So, this was the woman I'd be working for – me, who'd once gotten the award for best essay in year four, who'd met the governor general, who'd received one hundred US in prize money – money that paid for food for a few months in those days. Mama had been so relieved for the money because Daddy had left her high and dry, run away to Antigua with another woman – before he died of colon cancer. His comeuppance, Mama say.

Listen, is no secret that I don't too much like work. At eight, I had to sell peanut snacks across the trainline after school. Why I couldn't be like the children eating these snacks on their way home? I hate domestic labour and minding other people's children even more, so the longer I sat there, the more I knew accepting this job was my second big mistake.

The first big one was shacking up with Leroy, sometime deejay, moretime mechanic in Miami. I suppose this job was a reprieve from him, and it was his fault I missed the flight that bougie New Jersey lady booked for me.

It *was* all Leroy's fault. He say I was out of my mind if I think I could leave him for three whole months without cooking him some real meals, but when I put the lids on those containers of rice and peas and stewed chicken and finally got on the road to the airport, he insist on making a detour to his mechanic shop to see the progress on a truck they were repairing. So, I had to sit there in the passenger seat watching Leroy looking annoyingly attractive in his wife-beater and ripped jeans and talking long-long with a man in grease-splattered overalls.

Why had I come to this country when I had to rely on a man like Leroy or take whatever job I could get?

Leroy was never once serious about marriage. Did he think he could keep me under his thumb with fickle promises or threats of deportation?

Still, he did take care of the bills, and cooking him meals and having sex on his uneven mattress every so often – was that really so bad?

When Leroy finally dropped me off at the airport, I raced

to the gate but the counter agents damn near slammed the door to the jetway in my face. I didn't know whether it was relief or anger that washed through me.

Of course, the employer lady sound annoyed when I called to tell her about this development. Her voice sound higher than when she first tell me I could come for a trial.

"I really need someone. I can't find anyone at such short notice. I will just have to send you a train ticket instead."

I scowled at the phone. This rhatid woman never even want to sound like she Jamaican.

★

On the train to New Jersey, I was trying to convince myself that maybe working for someone was better than being with Leroy and wondering when my life would change.

Mama had given me money to fly out of Kingston three years before, not knowing that her dear daughter would spend the next three years with Leroy in his tiny Miami apartment and not entering any college – like Mama surely was telling the whole lane.

But as I watched the grey New Jersey streets whiz by, I couldn't help feeling this was going to be a ride down to rock bottom. As I say, I find the idea of cleaning up other people's shit or feeding their screaming offspring just too much. I told myself it was beneath me, but really it was because the year I turned fifteen I birthed and buried a baby. I was no longer the same.

But that's something I don't want to think about.

What I had to face was the fact I'd given up the dream of further schooling.

Maybe I learned to hate work because of Mama's example. She hadn't worked for years. She scammed foreigners out of their pensions with the promise of lotto millions. She was good at it. She never had to lift a broom again in another woman's household. Well, to me, even Mama's supposed non-work looked like hard work. She had to change her voice for different victims, pay strangers to collect incoming money at different Western Union places, and make hiding places for the money, like under a tile in the kitchen, so when the police raided our little one-floor home, there was nothing to find. Besides, the police had bigger fish to catch – the people who lived in the mansions that seemed to spring up over-night. They thought Mama was small fry caught up in some big scheme, and not its mastermind.

No. That was her thing, not mine, but maybe if I hadn't confided in her sister, Auntie Maxine – she lives in Fort Lauderdale and I thought she'd ask me to stay – I wouldn't be sitting on a train going to work for some uppity lady.

As the train jostled on, I remembered the first boy who'd caught my eye at fourteen. What a fool I was – the cliché girl believing herself in love for the first time. I was led away from simultaneous equations, to street corners and ganja, to bareback sex and being dumped. It was so long ago, but I still have to try not to think about the baby.

★

It was dark when I arrived in New Jersey. I walked out of the station toward the Escalade the woman had described. The vehicle was like the woman at the wheel: big, obnoxious, black. She insisted that I call her "Claire", but it felt better to just keep calling her "ma'am".

"Finally," the woman said, climbing out of the vehicle. "What an ordeal! But you are here now."

I smiled, hoping it didn't look too much like I was baring my teeth.

Claire took the small pulley from me.

"This is all you brought for three months?" she said as she tossed the little black bag into the back seat.

I did not respond and got into the front.

"This is my husband's, but you can use the minivan when you take the children out," the woman said, as we set off.

"Drive, ma'am?" I had not thought about this.

"You don't drive?" She said this in the same way she'd asked me why I didn't own a cellphone. "The moment I got here at twenty, I just had to get a driver's license. I don't know how you manage."

I let myself enjoy the warming seat and the light air coming in through the vents.

"So, Delvina, tell me about yourself? Why do you want to do this babysitting job?"

I glanced at the woman's profile, wondering how some-one who looked so ordinary could be so well off. She had an African-print scarf knotted at her forehead and a large white gold ring glistening on one of the fat fingers gripping the steering wheel.

"I took care of my younger siblings when my mother died."

I even surprised myself at how easily the lie came out – my mother as hearty as ever and me an only child. I wouldn't go near my young cousins when they came to visit us in St. James in the summer. I'd never do one thing to make their stay easier, not even when asked.

"Oh? Sorry to hear. So you like children, then?"

I pondered the question, watching cars flash by.

"Not all children, ma'am," I said. "I only like children who are at least four or five, who can say what's wrong with them and can feed theyself. They can answer when you call them, and they can play on them own."

Claire was crinkling her brow. Then, suddenly she laughed, a loud, long belly laugh punctuated with short, sharp intakes of air.

"For a moment, I thought you were serious," she said when she'd quieted down. "I have a nine-month-old and a two-year-old. I'm sure your aunt told you."

"Yes, ma'am," I said, meekly.

I had for once told the woman the honest-to-God truth.

I'd never dreamed of being a mother. I'd never wanted to hold a baby or smell the top of its head. I'd never played house or mommy or cook, not even when that fourteen-year-old boy breed me. I'd decided I would not keep his baby, especially when the boy shunned me the moment I told him. I decided I would not keep the baby, even if I had to throw myself off the roof into the ravine. I hoped that Mama would kill me – and save myself from having to do it.

Mama just said that I must remove my disgraceful self from the good-good Catholic school, that I would carry the baby to term, and get a job to support it – and that was all.

I did as I was told, and when the baby came, I named him Phillip, after my father – to spite Mama.

Like a cruel joke, Phillip lived for only three days, dying without no apparent cause.

I did not let them know how much I loved his squirming little body or how often I pressed my cheek against his to feel his warmth. After, I would cry and talk to my dead son when Mama was out of earshot. I still can't abide other people's offspring, even now.

When Claire turned the car off the main road it was into a lane of identical two-storey houses with tiny manicured lawns. I'd expected a wide yard and towering house with balconies and turrets. Did they count the trees in each yard and you had to get a special letter from the home owners' association if you wanted more than one, and bougainvillea instead of pine trees? I thought of the mango trees that sprang up in yards back home, pressing against the avocados and the coolie plum trees. And, oh God! The stringy mangoes you found everywhere with their juicy mouthfuls of fruit to suck down to their white hairy seed.

"So, will I have a day off?" I asked as the garage gate shut slowly behind us.

"Yes. One day a week. Maybe Sundays?"

"So, do I have to be in this house on my day off, or can I find a place to sleep away from here?"

I hadn't meant to be rude, but I didn't like how the woman's smile had now gone from her face.

"We will have to see," she said, handing me the pulley and rustling her keys.

My stomach contracted as we entered the house. It did seem bigger on the inside with ceramic tiles instead of wall-to-wall carpeting, like Leroy had in Miami.

"Andrea," the woman called, and a slender black woman came into the kitchen.

"Delvina, this is Andrea. We are so sad to see her go. She's abandoning us to go home for a bit." She looped her arm around Andrea's waist and put her head briefly on her shoulder. Andrea pulled away.

I immediately liked Andrea.

"She is such a treasure," Claire continued. "She will be here for a week, so she will sort of train you about how things run here."

"Okay, but can I go and lie down for a moment, ma'am?" I looked around for a room off the hallway.

"I suppose you must be tired," the woman said, as a man entered the kitchen. He was a little shorter than her, had a scraggly beard just under his chin and square-framed glasses perched on his nose. But quite pleasant to look at.

"Oh, Delvina, this is my husband, Richard," Claire said.

"Oh, hello, sir," I said.

"He will be around when you have to take your day off," the woman said.

I had not been good with woman folk, but seemed able to get on with men, especially older men like this Richard. I gave him a second look as he came across to greet me.

"Glad to have you, Delina," he said.

"Is Delvina, sir," I said. "With a 'v'."

"Let me help you with you bag." Andrea took the pulley from me.

"Yes, good thinking. Richard and I need to talk a little more."

I looked back at Richard and smiled. Then, I followed Andrea down the passageway.

"Them married twelve years and them just renew vows and everything," Andrea deposited the pulley in the room and I plopped down on the bed.

It was a much larger room than the one I shared with Leroy.

"Why you telling me that?" I said, removing my sneakers.

I began to like this helper less now.

"Because I have a feeling you is trouble. I know girls like you," Andrea said matter-of-factly.

"Girls like me?"

"Girls who fed up with them life and like to make mischief in other people marriage, just for the sport of it." Andrea folded her arms. "I like these people, and I don't want to hear that when I gone you destroy everything. I need this job."

"If the foundation weak, you can't blame the rain if it blow down everything," I said, reciting something Mama had said to a church sister who was condemning her for destroying the lives of people she did not know, people who might be living hand-to-mouth in America, but falling for her schemes. I lay back on the big queen-sized bed and looked up at the ceiling fan. "But I am not no rain. You don't haffi worry. I just here to get likkle money for a few months and go back from which part I come. Okay Andrea, dear?"

I did not like the sideways glance Andrea gave me as she left, but I brushed it off and curled up in the bed.

In a few moments, I could hear the muffled sounds of the woman and her husband talking on the other side of the wall. How was it, in this big house, they couldn't take their chatter to the other side, or, with all their money, make their walls thicker.

All I could hear was warbling, so I pressed my ear against the wall.

"I don't know about this girl," Claire, was saying.

"She seems like a nice sort – hard working."

"Richard, please tell me that you not seriously looking at this woman. I can't be thinking about that when I'm gone tomorrow," Claire said.

"When will you let that go? It was five years ago and nothing happened." Richard's voice rose through the walls.

I smiled. So, he had noticed me. I couldn't hear much else, except the words "responsibility" and "dedicated" coming out in snatches through the wall.

The travel debacle was beginning to take its toll on my limbs. I lay back on the bed and must have dozed off.

★

I opened my eyes to find myself in darkness. For a moment, I had forgotten where I was. A glance at my watch told me it was past midnight.

I wished I'd asked Andrea where to find the bathroom. The house was still when I poked my head into the passageway. Save a weak outside light spilling in through the window, everything was dark.

I found the bathroom at the end of the hall. Unbuckling my jeans I enjoyed plopping down on the cushioned toilet seat. As the steady stream of my urine broke the silence, I hoped I had not roused the house.

As I was using one of the little seashell soaps to wash my hands, it dawned on me what I had taken on. Was this my fate, to take care of someone else's children, working in someone else's house just as Mama had done before she found her own, albeit dishonest, means of survival?

But then eight years had passed since I buried little Phillip. Perhaps I was now ready for such a job. Perhaps I was stronger than I felt.

Perhaps.

Suddenly, the door swung open. I jumped.

"Sorry. Sorry," Richard said, pulling the door shut.

"No, I was done. You can come, man," I said.

It amused me the way he came in, sheepish, pulling his striped robe securely shut. What was the story behind Andrea's warning? Was Richard that susceptible to young women? Had some woman working in the house almost torn their marriage apart?

I suppose I really didn't have any reason to dislike Claire – she was giving me a job – but maybe it was like Mama said, "When your spirit don't take to somebody, nothing you can do can change it."

I lingered at the door, closed it with us both inside.

"I like that," I said, pointing to his striped robe. "I can touch it? Is cashmere?"

Richard looked a little younger without his glasses, and something about his scruffy looks made him more endearing.

I reached and touched it before he could object.

"Soft," I said, looking at him. I was close enough to touch him. "I like it." I watched his eyes descend to my mouth.

How easy it was. All I had to do was to press myself against him, slip my hand round the nape of his neck, and kiss him.

"Look, I have to go… badly," he said.

I stood there for a moment.

"That's okay," I said without turning to leave. "You can go."

"But without an audience," he said, tugging at the belt of his robe.

"Okay," I said smiling up at him. "I didn't eat anything from morning. Maybe we can get a late-night snack when you finish?"

I turned to walk away.

"Listen, I can't," he said, holding my shoulder to stop me.

"Can't what?" I said.

"I love my wife," he said. "Please close the door."

I felt the warmth climb up my neck.

"I was only playing. I not even that hungry," I said, and marched out from the bathroom.

★

I woke with a start. Claire was leaning over me, shaking me.

"Delvina, I am so sorry but this is not going to work out. Can you come to the kitchen?"

"What? What time is it?" I rubbed my eyes and sat up. "What I do, ma'am?"

"I will explain in the kitchen. Just get dressed and bring your bag with you."

When I came into the kitchen, Andrea was at the stove, and Richard was sitting at the dining table, not meeting my gaze.

"I'm going to pay for your ticket back to Miami, Delvina.

I am so sorry, but you not driving and not being able to verify if you should even be working here has made us reconsider the whole arrangement."

I looked over at Andrea methodically whisking eggs in a bowl and not meeting my eyes either.

"You think I want your crusty husband?" I said. "You really think I could do anything to make him want me if he didn't already want me from what him see just now?"

"Now come, miss," Richard started up, but broke off with one look from his wife.

"Here is the money for the ticket, and I put a little extra for your trouble," the woman said, extending the bills to me.

I looked at them, feeling the anger rise to my temples.

"You can keep your fucking money, ma'am," I said. "I have friends I can call to come and take me to the station. You sick if you think that I would want to work for you people anyway. Putting on airs. Thinking you better than ordinary folk."

"Delvina, you said you don't like children. You said you don't drive. These are not things that I agreed with your aunt."

"I just need a phone call and I will be gone," I said.

Andrea brought over the cordless phone. There was a smug look of pity on her face.

I snatched the phone out of her hands, seething. I did not need anybody's pity. In my handbag, I found my contacts book. I looked down the list, realising that most of them were from three years ago when I had just come to America, friends of Leroy, of Auntie Maxine, names of people who had settled all over. I found a Connecticut number. It must have been my aunt's college friend, Ms. Salina.

I turned my back and punched in the numbers and listened to it ring.

"It's no trouble at all, Delvina. We will get you a cab to the station and you can be on your way."

The phone continued to ring, then switched to the answering machine. I almost pretended that the woman had answered, but hung up.

"I will wait out on the corner for the cab," I said, grabbing the money that Claire held out.

I stopped at the doorway.

"If you so insecure, you should get some old hag to come take care of your brats," I said, "and not put decent people through this hassle."

As I stood on the sidewalk, I wondered whether I should have pretended and said I loved all children the same. Perhaps I should have said I could drive. I had not really wanted the job, but now I felt an old panic rising. What was I supposed to do? What would I tell Leroy?

I could always go home to Jamaica. I could just call Mama and tell her I was ready to come back.

That idea died. Mama had probably told the whole community how I was making it abroad. I had told her as much, leaving Leroy out of our talks.

I thought about asking Mama to send me some money. It would be novel for her to be sending money instead of receiving it. She would just have to get over the fact that her child had failed.

I looked back at the house, its walls cast in the warm pink glow of dawn. I felt alone looking at the yellow glow of light still coming from the kitchen and living-room windows. At least the woman would have to cancel her trip – or Ms. Andrea would.

Serve them right.

When I looked at the money in my hand, I realised the woman had given me five one hundred-dollar bills. I recounted it in disbelief. It was enough to stay in a motel for a week and a half at least.

Soon, a cab rolled up the drive.

I would call all the numbers in my little ruled book when I got to a phone. I would call Mama and tell her everything, but not to worry.

I would say that I had gotten a job as a waitress in New York – or even that I was going to audition as an actress.

No, Mama would not believe any of that.

I got into the back of the cab.

"Where to, ma'am?" the driver asked, leaning forward to adjust his radio.

I looked at the back of his head, his baseball cap and plume of smoke from his cigarette, but I did not really see him.

"I don't know," I said. "Just drive."

Something would turn up, I thought, as the car pulled out of the lane and merged with the early morning traffic.

COURT ROOM 5

Verona walks up to queue with the other accused waiting to go through the large wooden doors of Court Room number five. She feels the hand of the police officer on her shoulder and winces. Even through her clothes, his hand sears her. She looks down at the cold handcuffs around her wrists and tries to keep her breathing even.

On the other side of the door, she can hear a policeman rebuffing would-be spectators.

"No no no! No tube tops. No batty riders. No merinos. Is where you t'ink you going? Dancehall? You t'ink you can go before judge look so?"

Verona swallows hard as the doors open, and she files in behind three men, then slowly takes her place in the dock where a man already stands. She glances behind her to the gallery where every crevice seems filled with people, and her pulse quickens. Her body still smarts from the ordeal. She rubs her neck, still stiff from sleeping on the cold, hard bed in the police lock-up the night before. She is sure her clothes carry the pungent smell of urine from the cell.

The door opens again, and she looks around to see if it is her attorney. It is a man with a media badge around his neck; he clumsily bows and squeezes himself into the already overflowing front row of the seats to her left.

She looks up at the platform in front of her where the judge is already seated. She half expects to see him in a white curly wig like those judges in that English mini-series she used to watch with her grandmother in the good times when they lived together up in the hills of Lluiadas Vale. This judge at Half Way Tree Criminal Court is an unassuming figure in a simple black gown, but Verona does not miss the hard jaw and the grim stare he turns on those in the dock, and more pointedly at the man standing beside her.

"This is Edward Wilson from the church larceny case, Your Honour," the clerk of court is saying now, a tall, angular man in a muted black suit. Verona looks at the clerk's pants and notes the areas of shine – from what must have been excessive ironing. Her grandmother used to chastise her mother for such an error. It is something else to think about rather than what it means to be in the dock. Seeing Edward Wilson trembling a little does not help. Her mother must have come before a judge for offences such as these when Verona was not yet five, when they were put out of her grandmother's house over one of the many disagreements between mother and daughter.

"He is fully prepared to make restitution for his mistake, Your Honour," a stout woman in a black pants-suit is saying to the judge. She is at the same bench as the clerk, the only section of the courtroom not swollen with people.

Verona glances behind her again. She doesn't see anyone in the same school uniform as her own and lets out a little sigh of relief. She doesn't let herself think what it would mean if her arrest got back to the school, how the one steady thing in her life would be taken away. Then she spots the reporter again and her heart sinks.

"Was anything else stolen from the church?" the judge asks the clerk.

"A clock and two speakers," the clerk says, checking the file he holds. "He was also transporting a bag full of sweet

biscuits, bun, candy, and chewing gum – the remnants of a
recent church fund-raiser – when a watchman found him."

"Mr. Wilson, what do you have to say for yourself, sir?"
The judge's voice sounds worn-out and monotonous.

"Mi honour, is the rum my wife give me that day. I never
know it would have that effect on me, mi honour," he says.

"You are blaming your actions on drink?" the judge asks.
"Are you an alcoholic?"

"No no, mi honour. Is the one time and I never know it
would affect me so. Is like I lose my senses, but I not going
to do it no more if you could just gimme a chance – "

"He has no prior convictions," the lawyer interjects,
adjusting her glasses as she reads from a sheet of paper. "And
he has a wife and two small children. He is just a farmer that
fell on hard times."

"Well, Mr. Wilson, you say you won't do it again," the
judge says. "I can make sure of it. Stay with us a little."

He looks over at the clerk. "Remand for thirty days." He
pounds the gavel. "Next case!"

Verona feels that sound like a blow in her chest. She
doesn't look at the man as he is led away. She doesn't look
at the man in the media badge, but can tell from her
peripheral vision he is writing furiously on a pad of paper.
She focuses instead on the large stained-glass window to
the right of the room. No one is coming to defend her; her
mother is still probably on the steps of Scotiabank with her
hands outstretched, begging passers-by for spare change.
Verona saw her two days before as she passed on a coaster
bus heading to school. She had ducked down in shame.
She imagined her father was probably eating lunch in his
grand office overlooking Half Way Tree square right now,
unaware of her existence. She had even gone to Gordon
House, while parliament was in session, and waited for a

glimpse of him, wondering how to introduce herself. Did he remember the domestic helper he'd pitched out of his house for what her mother told her was a bogus claim of theft? He should help them now, take up his responsibility because that helper, her mother, was going mad again – even as she had begun to wonder whether her mother's story was true.

"Docket Number 29, female minor, Verona Samuels," the clerk of court drones.

Unshackled now, Verona rises and touches her frizzy cane-rowed hair, trying to smooth it with shaking hands. Her green school tunic and gingham shirt are both wrinkled.

"Charged with assaulting a police officer and resisting arrest, Your Honour," the clerk says. "Indecent exposure, malicious destruction of property and assault occasioning bodily harm."

There is a light ripple of laughter and comment from the gallery behind her.

"She?" "Look how she likkle-bit?" "Indecent exposure?" "Who she show her body?" "Who want to see?"

The judge glares at the gallery. Verona hangs her head. She wants only to crumple in her seat.

"And who is the arresting officer?" the judge asks.

"Corporal Fitz Bennet," the clerk says.

The man, Bennet, stands and in two strides is beside the clerk facing the judge. He is a large, balding man in a red-seamed police uniform with his arm in a sling.

Verona can still feel his hand on her, pressing her into the pavement. She tries not to look at him.

"And defence counsel?" the judge asks.

The clerk glances back at Verona.

"He does not appear to be here, Your Honour. A Mr. Roy Wellington."

"My auntie husband say him would represent me, sir," Verona said in a small voice, "Him don't reach as yet."

She does not add that it was not her real aunt, but a neighbour who'd started taking her in three years ago, when her mother was regularly going missing. The shame had washed over her when Mrs. Wellington came by the fence with a bowl of rice and stewed peas, or a bag of mangoes, or school supplies like the grade four reader her mother forgot to rent from the school. At first she'd resisted, telling the neighbour she was fine, even as her belly growled, even when Mrs. Wellington's son, who was in her class at school, would brandish his new composition books at the start of the school year, and she continued to use the dog-eared ones from the previous term. She had hated the sight of the woman's perfectly curled hair – her curlers worn as they should be at night – unlike her mother who never took them off on days when she was too tired and sad to speak. Perhaps she should be grateful that Mrs. Wellington did not call the police nor alert the Child Protection and Family Services Agency to report what could only be seen as her mother's neglect.

Verona had only accepted the woman's charity when she could no longer withstand her hunger, when she needed to borrow the textbook the woman's son used, and when her mother disappeared from the lane for longer and longer stretches. When her mother returned, occasionally, they would go back to their sparse, dark house, and use candles until her mother could get the lights turned back on.

"I going to get something for the table," her mother had said one time after she collected her, and Verona knew this was because she'd seen the large bowl of otaheite apples on the Wellington's kitchen table.

"Why we mustn't have something for our table as well?"

her mother had said. All the things Verona wanted to say bubbled up in her neck and stayed there, so she only sighed and nodded.

When neither her mother nor bowl nor fruit turned up that night, Verona went next door and watched School Challenge Quiz on the Wellington's large screen TV. Mr. Wellington, who had not spoken much to Verona before this, patted her head and called her quick as a whip when she knew all the science, mathematics, and history answers.

So perhaps she should not have cursed Mrs. Wellington when she called her mother a "careless woman" for leaving her daughter so often to fend for herself. It was not, after all, anything that Verona had not thought herself. Perhaps it was because her mother looked so small and worn as she stood in the doorway, and Mrs. Wellington shook her head and murmured, "That woman is just too careless", that something had snapped.

Anger had risen up her neck and pulsed at her temples.

"And what you know about our troubles? Why you feel you can just take over just 'cause I need your help a few times. My mother soon be okay. We don't need you no more!"

Verona could still see the curious display of disappointment and pity in the woman's eyes. Had her anger really been meant for this woman and not the one who stood in the doorway, who had come back to take her to an empty house, to hunger pains so sharp they felt like knife wounds, to hiding under the bed when the landlord threatened eviction for the third time that month if he didn't get his money?

So, after her arrest a week later, it had taken all Verona's will to call Mrs. Wellington from the lock-up. She knew with a pang there was no one else to call, no one else who would care enough to help.

At the other end of the line, Mrs. Wellington had seemed

silent for an eternity. Verona wondered if she had put down
the phone and walked away. Then Mrs Wellington said she
would ask her husband to help; he was a solicitor, but he
only dealt with taxes and civil matters, so she could not
make Verona any promises.

"Let us deal with these three men here and maybe your
attorney will see fit to pay us a visit," the judge says now.

Verona releases a ragged breath, sits back down, and
watches the corporal retake his seat. She stares at him,
squeezed between the two plain-clothed policemen in
washed-out plaid shirts. He doesn't smile at her in the way
that made her go cold when she was in the lock-up. He looks
at her deadpan and then turns back to the judge.

She has grown up to distrust the police. She thinks of
how her mother cursed them the year after they left Lluiadas
Vale and she had been arrested for possession of stolen
household goods – like the sunflower bedspread she'd
given Verona, the pots and the very curtains in their front
window – all taken from the supermarket where she worked
as a cashier.

"Me will give them back. I do it all for my daughter, sah,
Please!" her mother had wailed.

It was then that Verona had wondered how much of what
her mother told her about her father was real, for there she
was lying to the officer. None of what her mother had done
felt like it was done with her in mind. Was any of it true? Was
the man with the streak of white in his hair and the perfect
suit she had watched on television debating with the oppo-
sition minister of finance, was he really her father?

Verona had watched her mother being taken away and
vowed never to ape her actions. Her mother somehow
escaped jail then, and this isn't lost on Verona now as she sits
awaiting her turn in this stuffy little court room.

Two men, identical twins it seems, stand up in the dock beside her, one named Rohan, and the other, Ryan. They are jointly accused of possessing ganja. Verona is only half listening now, watching the door to see if Mr. Wellington will come, and if Mrs. Wellington will be there in the gallery of spectators.

She almost doesn't want them to come.

She tells herself she doesn't need them.

The brothers, the clerk is saying, were caught trying to smuggle roasted breadfruit stuffed with two kilograms of compressed ganja through the Norman Manley International Airport.

"Guilty, but with some explanation, please. Is a man name Jim give us the breadfruit-dem to send go to foreign, Your Honour," the first one, Rohan, says.

"Yes, Jim," the other, Ryan, chimes in.

"But they were found in your possession," the judge says.

"Yes, yes, your greatness," Rohan says, and some spectators behind them cackle. "And is our first offence, my lord. We really trust this Jim, judge, but him lie to us."

"Yes, Jim," Ryan parrots again.

"Is that all you can contribute?" the judge asks.

Ryan looks at his brother for a moment.

"I not sure, my lord," Ryan says, finally.

Verona cannot join in the waves of laughter spreading through the courtroom. She barely hears the clerk call them all to order again. She cannot quell the sinking feeling in her chest. Perhaps she deserves to be here for having spat her ingratitude in the face of a woman who was only trying to help, for being born to a woman given to erratic behaviour, neglect and comas of grief. Perhaps it was something she did as a child, something she cannot now fix.

"Well, unfortunately, you both, and not this Jim, will

have to pay the seven thousand dollars fine and be re-manded for ninety days," the judge says, slamming down his gavel again.

Verona tries to shake off how quickly these men are dealt with, handcuffed again, and led away.

Before she can think, she is the only one remaining in the dock.

"We need to move forward," the judge says, looking at Verona again. "Stand up, young lady. How do you plead?"

"Not guilty," she says in a little voice.

"Speak up!"

"Not guilty!"

Corporal Bennet is once again facing the judge, adjusting one of the chevrons on his uniform with the hand which isn't bandaged.

"What are the allegations, Corporal?"

"Your Honour, on the fifteenth day of February, two days ago, I stopped a coaster bus carrying school children in Half Way Tree Square. At approximately 10:05 a.m., I inspected the driver's papers and found he had no insurance and was driving on an expired license, so I informed all passengers to disembark from the vehicle because the bus was to be impounded, but the accused refused to leave the vehicle. I warned her that I would have to bodily remove her, Your Honour."

Verona hangs her head as Bennet speaks.

"She had to be restrained by myself and my partner, Corporal Wilkins, because she was resisting us, Your Honour. As I placed her on the ground to handcuff her, she bit me on the finger and the wrist and tried to choke me. That is how I sustained this injury to my shoulder and neck."

Bennet holds up his index finger in a bandage and points to his arm in a sling. Verona fidgets. How can she tell the judge that perhaps it was seeing her mother through the bus window that had undone her, how the injustice of it had made the blood rush to her head when the uniformed men made their demands?

"Then, when she was taken to the lock-up, she tear off her tunic and say that she know her rights and no police could frisk her while she in her drawers."

The laughter erupts again.

"I will clear the court room if you continue to make this a spectacle! Control yourselves," the judge says firmly.

"Then, she threatened me several times, Your Honour."

"You is a liar!" Verona shouts.

The hush seems to hold her frozen in that moment, one damning hand raised and aiming at the large man and her face taut in an odd mix of anger and confusion.

"Ms. Samuels, you will get your turn to give evidence," the judge says. "You do not conduct yourself in this way in my court room. I will have you removed from the room!"

Verona looks down at her knuckles gripping the rail of the dock, feels the bone twitching in her temple.

"There was a large crowd gathering, and they were encouraging the accused to fight us," the Corporal says. "It took three officers to restrain her."

"Young lady, are you denying these allegations?" the judge asks. "Think carefully before you respond."

Verona looks at the reporter scribbling in his pad and hopes that her name will not appear in print, that just turning sixteen two weeks before means they have to keep her name out of the papers.

"Yes… and no, Your Honour," she says finally.

"I hope you realise this is a serious matter, young miss," the judge cautions.

"I know, Your Honour," she says quietly, "but he lying. I never do none of them things."

Then with a heavy sigh, she says, "I want to change my plea to guilty with explanation."

The judge pauses for a moment.

"Oho. So can you describe to me what happened?"

"This police was jus' pulling and shoving us schoolers off the bus, and I said that him don't have to behave so toward us just because we are schoolers," she says. "Then, him box me across my face and pull me off the bus. That was when I resist them because they were being unfair, sir."

"That is a blatant lie, Your Honour," Bennet says with a bemused smile. "My partner was right there and can vouch for me. She tried to *choke* me."

"And I only take off my clothes in the guardroom to warn them because I know people what get rape by a policeman right thereso in the station. I did want everybody to know them couldn't try that with me," Verona says.

Just then, the doors open and a man in a dark tweed suit bustles in.

"Sorry, Your Honour," he says and gives a hurried bow before stepping into the bench with the clerk and the two other lawyers. "I am Roy Wellington and I am defending this accused."

"Mr. Wellington, your client has just admitted to assaulting the officer and the charge of indecent exposure."

"One minute to confer with her, Your Honour?" Mr. Wellington asks.

The uniformed police are taking five shackled men into the dock.

"We have several other cases to get through before 3 p.m., sir, so be quick about it," the judge says with a wave of his hand.

Mr. Wellington turns to Verona and whispers, "Why you change you plea? You want to get lock up? You have to let me fix this, now."

Verona is not sure how to respond. She looks over at the corporal. The old anger is surfacing. She thinks of the night spent in the lock-up. She thinks of the female constable gruffly putting back on her clothes. She remembers the sting from the corporal's baton. She remembers the feeling of helplessness.

After a few more words of reprimand, Mr. Wellington turns back to the judge.

"Your Honour, I would like to have these charges against my client dismissed. It is clearly a case of police brutality, and my client was acting in self-defence. She is a good student, Your Honour, who has never had any run-ins with the law. She will sit five CXC subjects in a few months and is an active member of her community."

The judge motions to the clerk and is handed the file.

"Miss Samuels, you want the court to believe that the police restrained you without cause?"

"Your Honour…" she starts, but falls silent, then tries again. "Your Honour, he don't have the right to hit us, to beat us down like we is animals. They supposed to protect us."

Her voice trembles with the tears at the back of her throat. An image of her mother standing there on the steps comes to her.

"They supposed to protect us," she says again.

"Your Honour, Ms. Samuels has been through a lot in the past few months," Mr Wellington says. "My wife and I have been taking her in while her mother is… away."

The judge regards her for a moment, his face unmoving.

"Ms. Samuels, considering that you have admitted to assaulting the policeman, I believe you are culpable in some way in this matter. But given that this is your first offence, you are fined seven thousand dollars and one-year probation. You will need to do some community service to be completed at this police station. You will need to check with me periodically. Clerk?"

The clerk looks down at his large book.

"March 3," he says.

"Return on March 3 and try to stay out of trouble 'til then."

"Yes, your Honour," she says, stepping from the dock.

Verona thinks that the judge could well have said a million dollars for all she could do to get the money together. Every time she was able to save a few dollars from the money given to her by the Wellingtons, her mother would find it, money that could have paid for at least one of her CXC exams.

As she is led away, Verona looks behind her at the gallery. Mrs. Wellington has not come.

"Lying bitches, these young girls nowadays," Corporal Bennet murmurs as Verona passes him.

She stills the urge to spit in his face. She knows that spitting even at his feet as she walks by will have her marched back to the dock with fresh charges. She wishes she could just turn and smile at his words, but she looks back at the clerk who has put her file away.

"Next case," she hears the judge say. She catches the same drawn expression on his face. She looks back at the people in the gallery whose attention has shifted to the five accused now standing in the dock.

No one seems to notice her as she is led out of the courtroom.

MELBA

From the kitchen, Melba saw the upturned soles of Edgar's water boots and knew instantly he was dead. The realization spread cold through her chest, but for the next five minutes, she stood paralysed at the sink and watched the water pour over the Pyrex dish in which she had made the macaroni casserole they had just eaten together.

They had sat across from each other chewing wordlessly. He had long since stopped complimenting her on the cooking, and even that had been the extent of their dinner conversation over the last ten years. Once, Melba began lamenting how the principal at her elementary school still went over her teaching plans more than she did those of the other teachers; she was certain it was because she was the only black, Caribbean woman on the staff. Edgar had complained that too much talking interfered with his digestion, so, thereafter, they mostly ate in silence.

Melba's husband of thirty years had always been a man of few words, though when the house was full of the noise of children, it had bothered her less. They had come from Jamaica in 1985, newly married – just less than six weeks. She had left her job at a small school in Mandeville to follow him to Florida, then New York and now they were settled in Louisiana, he now a retired contractor.

When the accident had taken her fourteen-year-old Eliza

and sixteen-year-old Phillip, Melba and Edgar no longer knew what to say to each other.

She dried her hands and went out to where he lay by the rose bush. She looked down on him, his hands slack around the hose that spewed water around his head.

This was where they had sprinkled the ashes of their children and Edgar had insisted on planting canna lilies and roses. They never spoke about the accident, but argued about burial or cremation. Melba was Pentecostal and Edgar had abandoned the Presbyterian faith of his childhood, but, in the end, the practicality of cost decided it and their children became, as Melba thought, manure for roses.

A reporter had taken a quote from them after the memorial service for what the media was calling "The School Bus Tragedy".

Edgar had deferred to Melba. She had said simply, "It is the worst feeling to bury a child. Far worse to bury two."

They had been one of many parents left to rebuild their lives. The man who drove his pick-up into the bus died instantly, and Melba had thought this a small mercy that his name would live no longer than her children. She would grieve for her children. The man would meet his maker. That was that.

She retrieved Edgar's straw hat lying a few feet away, held it in her hands for a moment, looked down on his weathered face and began to weep quietly. Edgar had been a stubborn man who shunned doctors and concocted his own medicines, despite Melba's warnings. A few years before, she had seen him hold his chest, and he reluctantly conceded to her prodding to go to a walk-in. She remembered his gruff resignation when they told him he was at a high risk of a heart attack. He waved it off as the result of Melba overcooking the beef every Wednesday.

She snapped out of her trance, ran back inside, and called an ambulance. They found her lying beside him, shrieking and pummelling his chest. She was not one to shout hallelujahs and get in the spirit when in church, so hysterics did not come naturally to her. The paramedics naturally interpreted her actions, her clutching his chest, getting mud on her clothes and fighting them for the body, as grief at the loss of her husband.

They did not realize she wept for herself. She was neither wife nor mother now.

In the beginning she had loved Edgar, from the moment he stood at the doorway of her grade six classroom in Mandeville, asking directions to the principal's office. Their courtship had been brief. She had distracted him from his work as a construction worker on the new school site, and their talking in the hallway had parlayed into trips to the cinema and concerts in Mandeville square.

As the years ebbed, she loved him less. He let the thing between them die from neglect, often becoming sullen without provocation. He changed even more after they started their new life in America, becoming less and less the man who wooed her with notes, june plums and hibiscuses. In America began the pulling away.

Once, early in their marriage before the children, when they lived in rundown apartment in the Bronx, she had followed him to a bar, imagining that he had lovers, brash black American women on the block who loved his accent and workman's build, but instead she found him sitting by himself, nursing white rum, his face drawn. She did not feel any more relieved. Perhaps it would have been better had he been with another woman. Hate was far more satisfying than worry.

"Is what, Eddie?" she had asked one night, when she

found him sitting in their darkened living room. "Something happen at work? You want us go back home?"

There was something almost hopeful in her voice.

"Is nothing, love," he said. "Go back to bed."

"Edgar, tell me. We can go away. Somewhere."

She came and sat beside him on the sofa.

"I don't want to go away. Plus, we cannot afford it right now, and we don't have anything back home. This is where we live now, Mel." He patted her hand.

It was true. Between them, they had one relative, Edgar's elderly aunt, Ruthie McDermott, who lived in New York, who had made it possible for him to live in the States permanently.

"This is where we live now," he said quietly and kissed her forehead.

Melba was not assuaged by this, but she decided to leave him be. As she got up, she felt his hand on her leg. She turned back and his hands encircled her waist, and he slowly pulled up her polyester nightdress and brought her flush against him. She wrapped her hands around him, and kissed him tentatively, holding her breath, willing this fleeting intimacy to last. She marvelled that when they came together, he knew how to make her feel safe, yet their lives diverged as soon as his body left hers. As they rocked together, she kissed him and felt his face wet against hers. It was a wonder to be this close to him and yet be unable to comfort him.

When he succumbed to whatever torment he was enduring, he would pull away, even in spirit. She would often find him weeping, like this, at night. She would pretend not to notice, to preserve his pride, even as it ate away at her.

Then, when the world was already becoming unbearable for them, a drunk driver slammed into the school bus carrying thirty children, turning it over and killing everyone.

Their world stopped; now they lived in tandem with each other, yet wholly apart.

★

It was two weeks after Edgar's funeral that it started. She got on the Lafayette city bus after doing the shopping and just did not get off it again until all the buses stopped running for the evening. Edgar had been the one to drive their station wagon, so it sat in their driveway and she took the city bus.

It was on her way to the corner store that it struck her that she did not have to rush home. She had gotten up at dawn, shredded sweet potato to make the pudding that Edgar enjoyed on Sunday afternoons, then realized that Edgar was not going to come in from the garden to enjoy it.

She looked out of the bus window at the lots of miniature plantation-style houses. It always amused her that here many Americans did not have gates but hedges to mark their territory. That would not have worked in Spanish Town back home. There, some people had concrete fences and two-sided grills on their windows.

In the store, she picked up and put down a large bag of rice. When would she ever prepare this much rice again?

On the way home, when she reached the stop before hers, she knew she would not get off.

The lane leading to her green door came and went. The bus jostled along and when it stopped, Melba watched with a strange fixedness as people boarded and disembarked. She stayed on until the bus completed the route and returned to the terminus. There she got on the Number 65 because it was the longest route.

She did the same thing the next day and the next.

When she was at the house, she thought only about

joining her family nestled out there. Edgar's ashes were in the garden with the children's. He had not wanted to be buried, so she and three others – an elderly white man she did not quite know, Frazier from Baton Rouge who had worked alongside Edgar at the construction business for fourteen years, and Melba's neighbour, Phillis, who had tried without much success to befriend Melba – sent off Edgar without fanfare. She had admonished him to take care of the children, and released his ashes to the wind.

At night, she had dreamed repeatedly about falling into a bed of thorns. She would wake up, calling out for Edgar, then wept until she fell asleep again, often as the sun rose.

On the bus, there was space to think about other things. As a girl she had ridden the bus from Zephyrton to Brunswick Avenue and felt calmed by the early morning fog blanketing everything. Somehow, life seemed more bearable when the scenery was transient. She imagined taking trips to Boscobel and Port Royal. She would rent a little house near the sea and grow scotch bonnet pepper and pak choy as her mother did when they lived in Clarendon.

She wanted to go back even though she felt a traitor of sorts, having sworn allegiance to the stars and stripes all these years ago. Edgar had always promised that they would go back when he turned sixty-five and retired. But she had also heard about the fate of some returning residents, whom unscrupulous people had preyed on, those who watched the number of barrels a person claimed at the wharf, or learned how long they had been away. Some had turned up in the marshland with their throats cut.

So they had decided not to build that house on the south coast as they had dreamt in the warmth of early love. They had been frugal, planning for college tuitions that would never be used, denying themselves annual vacations back home. In rare good humour, Edgar would joke about owning a private beach in Jamaica in their golden years, that their children were his investment; they would be a judge, a doctor.

"Jamaica go always be there, Mel," Edgar had said to her, while she breastfed two-month old Phillip one August evening.

"But I want to show Phillip where him really come from," she had said, smiling down at the pudgy infant.

"Phillip is American, plus this is an election year and you know how fool Jamaican people behave when MP full up them head with promises."

The next year Jamaica was once again out of reach. Edgar complained that family expenses were "bleeding him dry".

The next year they did visit Jamaica when Edgar's aunt died from heart failure. She had instructed them that she was to be interned at Bethel Church of God in Westmoreland where she had tithed for many years, even after she had moved to Brooklyn. But Aunt Ruthie had died in debt and Edgar had to bear the weight. It made him surlier than ever.

Melba held the memory close of those seven days, watching Phillip, now two-years-old, try his little teeth on jackass corn, enjoy soursop and otaheite apples, and play on a beach in Lucea. She knew he would have no memory of it but, just watching, she felt she had been given a gift. They had come down during Jonkunu season and, towards the end of the trip, even Edgar had softened – being affectionate, holding Phillip on his shoulders as they danced to mento and calypso and reggae and watched the effigies of past prime ministers and national heroes in the parade. This time he was not wilting from his wife's arms around him. Would it have been better to have stayed? They went back four times before the children died but they never reclaimed that jubilance and ease with each other they had had in those early days.

★

On the fourth week of Melba's bus escapades, with her all-day pass in her hand, she boarded the number 45 and took her usual window seat at the very rear of the bus. She had begun to see some passengers regularly and thought perhaps it was their population of this moving world that made her forget her own loneliness. She had secretly named them, though she was sure they hardly saw her, a grey-haired woman with cream sandals, peasant skirts and calico beads, watching them.

The woman who came on from the corner of East St. Mary Boulevard and Johnston, like clockwork at noon every day, was "Miss Inez" in Melba's mind. She wore a black apron, black baseball cap and was gaunt and angular – like a woman of the same name who worked at the tuck shop in Melba's Mandeville school. Then, "Ralph" would come clattering into the bus with his signs, his trombone, his dirty pants and makeshift straw hat. She had seen him playing downtown with the hat face up in front of him, just like the street performers she had seen on the subway in New York. She had known a Ralph once, who took her virginity behind the star-apple tree and never spoke to her again. She liked to think that this was how he ended up, relying on the generosity of strangers. Other passengers merged together, like the students pouring in at the stop just outside the university. They, though, made her think too much about how, had they lived, Eliza would be a sophomore in college and Phillip at graduate school.

As the bus coasted along the airport road, Melba watched a distant aircraft's ascent with a pang. She was beginning to tire of this meaningless traipsing up and around the sleepy town. She would go back to the little green door of the house that Edgar built.

There was nothing to go home to Jamaica for. She no longer knew anyone. Here, at least, in Lafayette, the hated garden still held her loved ones; to leave would feel also like an abandonment. Perhaps she could find work. Just fifty-seven, she was still strong. She had experience in school systems in Jamaica and Lafayette.

Melba looked up and found the female bus driver fur-rowing her brows at her in the rear-view mirror.

"Not getting off today again, baby?"

Melba looked around and realized she was alone. She hated how grown people in this town called strangers "baby" and "honey" with a familiarity that she could not bring herself to reciprocate.

"No. No. Is fine."

She had not realized that anyone had noticed her unusual habit, and hoped the woman would not pry. Thankfully, the bus merged again with the traffic.

"You not from here," the driver shouted, again glancing at her and then back at the road. It was not a question.

Melba did not welcome this intrusion; it opened up a line of questioning she found exhausting. It particularly irked her when people said she did not "sound" Jamaican. She still had, she knew, a very thick Trelawney accent, but they would be hard pressed to understand her if she spoke to them the way she would to a fellow countryman.

Today, Melba did not feel inclined to participate.

"No. Not from here," she replied, and looked out of the window.

"I could tell." The woman was grinning, but Melba did not smile at her. She noted instead the way she wore her hair in four plaits. It reminded her of a woman she used to buy yellow yam from in Mandeville market every other Saturday. Somehow that made her dislike her more.

The woman seemed to be waiting for a response, but graciously did not continue the conversation. When the bus turned into the terminus, Melba got off. She felt wearier than usual. It was only noon, but she would go home and turn in.

"Bye now," the bus driver said, extracting herself from the driver's seat.

Melba waved a thin hand.

"Wait," the woman said. "You left your bag, here, baby."

The driver walked to where Melba had sat and picked up a blue canvas bag and handed it to her.

"Wait, you worked at the DaCosta School?" the woman asked, looking at the school named etched on the bag.

"No," Melba said.

She couldn't believe she had taken up that bag of all bags that morning. Melba stepped off the bus. The woman followed.

"My daughter went to that school," she said. "She died in the school bus accident in '01."

Melba looked at her, amazed at how easily the words came out.

"Sorry to hear that," she said, simply.

She noticed they were walking in the same direction.

"What was her name?" Melba asked, feeling trapped by the conversation, but still somewhat intrigued.

"Sarah, after my mother," the woman said. "She was such a bright little girl. Really good at her figures."

"I lost two that day," Melba said before she could stop herself. It felt strange to say it out loud after so long. She thought how she had wanted to say it to Edgar. *We lost our babies*, she would have said. *We need to talk about them.*

"Two at once?" the woman said, stepping back. "I couldn't imagine losing all of my other children like that."

"Yes. Phillip and Eliza," Melba said, her voice softening. "Phillip was good at figures, too. He didn't get it from me. That was his father, my husband, Edgar."

Melba turned the calico beads around and around on her wrist.

"He died a few weeks ago," she said.

"Oh my dear," the lady kept saying. "Oh my dear."

"Eliza could sing," Melba said, brightening again. "She would sing around the house and drive my husband crazy with it. She would have got private lessons if we had the money."

"That's the thing," the woman said. "But I'm sure she knew you loved her. I'm sure they both knew you loved them."

Melba nodded.

Melba started when the woman hugged her.

"Listen, I need to go, but you should come by the Baptist church right around the corner on Jefferson," she said. "Ask for Miss Linda, okay, baby?"

Melba nodded again.

She watched the woman disappear into the transit office and found she was crying. The tears were spilling out of her, but she somehow felt lighter.

She walked toward the Number 30 bus. It would take her to the lane that led to her green door.

There were some things she needed to say to Edgar.

THE BLACKOUT

Paboo thrust his shovel into the red earth and dumped the dirt on a growing mound, then took a swig of white rum from his flask.

"At this rate, we not going to dig the lady grave before is time," Straight Finger grumbled, shovelling feverishly.

Paboo passed the flask to Crebe, grabbed a clump of citronella and rubbed it on his ankles to keep the mosquitos away.

"Every time you stir up the earth, you must also take a drink. Everybody know that," Paboo said. "That way the spirit don't rise up and follow we."

Crebe took a drink, wiped his mouth, and handed the flask back to his friend.

"And why you think we ask you fi come?" Paboo said to Straight Finger.

"Yes. We could-a share the money between we two, but we need fi make sure is three, not two digging grave. Everybody know is odd number must dig grave when a full moon forming," Crebe said.

"That is pure nonsense," Straight Finger said, but stopped shovelling to look up at the sky that was beginning to grow mauve and orange with the coming dusk. The leaves of the breadfruit tree hung menacingly over where they stood in the graveyard. In less than an hour, they would carry the body out from the church.

"And is a nasty woman in life, so I don't wish to see her in no demon form," Crebe said, bending to dig another shovelful of earth.

Straight Finger watched them with disgust, shook his head and began to shovel once again.

"And why they do the service so late that we have to be out here digging now and not in full daylight?" Straight Finger complained.

"I suspect them want to get rid of the body as soon as possible," Crebe said.

"You sure right," Paboo said with a snort.

Henry Boudan, known as "Boo" from his school days, had become "Paboo" now that grey hairs were sprouting at his temples. His friend from those days, born Christopher Beres, had long been "Crebe". They were rarely away from each other.

More than one teacher had told them they were lucky to have graduated at all from school and he did not see much in their future but skylarking and mischief. Paboo was not one to challenge such wisdom and went straight from school to work on his father's yam patch, only to be banished for making sloppy uneven paths in the field, for sleeping in the bush or stealing away to help himself to Ms. Upton's mangoes and ackee. If he wasn't being a nuisance there, he was embroiled in a money game of dominoes he hardly ever won. Before long, Paboo's father put him out of the house, saying that his mother, buried out under the June plum trees from when Paboo was eight, would be turning in misery to learn what her son had become.

Crebe had it even harder. While he had managed to escape the worst kinds of abuse at the so-called place of safety where he'd been placed, he didn't avoid the routine beatings "to straighten out the boys-dem." For years, both he and Paboo had moved from pillar to post until they found a squat in a ramshackle wooden dwelling where the new pastor stored wood and tools to repair the crumbling church. Though new, the minister was a very old man they dubbed Methuselah because of his shock of white hair, bent frame, and refusal to retire. He left them to themselves as long as they dug the graves and performed other tasks that did not require too much brain power. They had been doing this now for ten years.

"Is probably a patoo she-a go turn into," Crebe said, resting his weight on the hilt of his shovel. "She go become some night bird since is nighttime she dead and bury inna."

Straight Finger, who had shovelled four times as much as Paboo and Crebe combined, shook his head. Then, he too stopped to rest and rubbed the stiffened index finger on his right hand from which he got his name.

"You two whey believe in duppy, don't know the first rule is not to talk ill of the dead," he said. "Besides, is how Ms. Mavis dead, though? I hear so much different story."

Paboo chuckled without mirth, his head beginning to swim with the alcohol.

"Is the night of the black out," he said, looking back at the church.

That night, Mavis had come down the lane like an ominous cloud glooming over everything, so even the stray dog made himself scarce. It was pitch black, the electricity outed. The pastor had instructed Paboo and Crebe to cut down an old guava tree that threatened to bring down the wires any time there was a hurricane. But as they felled it, its branches did just that and with a spark and pop the lights went out. Now Mavis was on the warpath. They knew she was coming, not because of the flash of her white cotton head-tie illuminated in the moonlight, but because her shrill voice reached the group huddled around the flashlight at the foot of the hill long before she was fully visible.

"Is which monkey business you keeping up with, Pastor?" She was breathless with anger, puffing out the words with each step.

Paboo had held the light up, casting the pastor's face in a grim white light.

Mavis tripped over the fallen branches as she came closer.

"Watch your step," the pastor said belatedly.

"Me did know the tree was too near the power line, but him wouldn't listen," Crebe said.

Sighing heavily, the pastor stooped and began clearing the fallen branches out of the way.

"Well, it knock out the transformer clean-clean," Mavis said.

"So nobody up your way have light?" Distress crinkled the pastor's weathered face.

"Nobody! No light from here all the way up to the hill to the main road."

"This was not how I saw all my efforts going," the pastor said. The very thing he had tried to prevent had come to pass.

"So now all my food mus' spoil because you decide fi cut down tree before you call the correct authority? Why you decide to do this at night of all times? Cho!"

Paboo felt some guilt at that. He and Crebe had disappeared during the day after overhearing the pastor discussing the guava tree. Paboo had no strong feelings about it either way. He just wanted to avoid having to work under the sun. The tree had stopped producing the fat yellow fruit he and Crebe had enjoyed, so he'd agreed to its destruction.

It was probably true what some church people said – that the tree had stopped bearing after a seer woman named Mama Myrtle was buried there.

"Nothing we can do til morning," the pastor said as he got to his feet again.

"You need to do something," Mavis said. "Just know the church paying for everything I lose out that house."

"I sure your appliance dem are quite okay, Ms. Mavis," the pastor said.

"I carrying all a you to court, you hear? Jus' wait."

More people had come down to the bottom of the hill with their flashlights. They formed what looked like a strange wake for the fallen tree, the pastor standing over it, shaking his head.

"Why you always the first to challenge everything I doing on church grounds, eh?" the pastor demanded of Mavis. "From ever since I come to this here church, you the first one grumbling, grumbling all the livelong day."

"Look around. We in darkness, Pastor. How you expect we mus behave? And you two stooges just stand up like *bafhan* and mek him do this?"

Paboo thought how much she had soured, lines of rage and worry rippling across her forehead. The girl he'd courted in their school days was long gone.

Then he had liked Mavis's sharp tongue – when it lashed anyone but him. Even Crebe had felt its sting, for it was no secret that she was sweet on Paboo and him alone. At first, taking her to neck behind the school chapel had been pure sport, but he began to like her little round eyes laughing only for him. She would not put up with the other boys, who, whenever she rebuffed them, claimed she was spreading her rump in secret for every man in the lane.

"You taste sweet like passion fruit," he would tell her and, at first, Mavis did not mind his rough ineloquence. Despite her mother telling her she must never offer herself, Mavis had succumbed to him. She had quickly learned that, for all his talk, Paboo knew very little about sex or girls. Their dalliance had been as brief as her patience with such ignorance.

"What you doing after you leave school?" she had asked him once, when they were lying together half naked in the banana grove.

He was breathing heavily, still feeling embarrassed that he had fumbled through the whole thing, and she had told him they could try again in a few moments, when she had recovered from his awkward, ardent thrusts.

"I don't have no real plans," he had said.

Perhaps he could have predicted the end of their involvement by the way she sighed, pulled on her panties, and said she had to go home before her mother sent the lane out to find her.

"I going away after school anyway," she said. "I been meaning to tell you."

"Where? To foreign?" He tried to mask the apprehension in his voice.

"Yes. I have some family over in Connecticut," she said. "Things easier there, them say."

Paboo hated to admit how crestfallen he was at the news. He could only account for her ambition through her obsession with the old magazines her mother brought back from the salon where she rented a chair as a part time hair stylist. He'd watch Mavis pore over the white models in the catalogues and photos of the syndicated soap stars with their brilliant white teeth and perfectly coiffed hair. She wanted a job in an office, to wear button-up shirts with little puffed sleeves and frills down the front, and pumps with the heels like those in the magazines – not too high or anything – practical but fashionable. She would be somebody.

When she left suddenly before the end of the school year, wagging tongues said it was because she had become pregnant and gone up into bush country to have the baby, but Paboo was not convinced. How could he think that when he had barely gotten all the way inside her in the few times she let him try the thing, and he did not believe she had been opening herself to the other boys, no matter what they said.

When she returned for a visit in the summer looking rosy and plump, he wondered. When her mother, Pearl, supposedly became pregnant at the age of forty-two, while Mavis was away, and then gave birth to a daughter she called Petronella just after Mavis returned, doubt began to form.

When Mavis walked up the street, he hid himself, cursing his cowardice. In her bright floral dress, her skin clearer and glowing, it certainly looked like things were easier in Connecticut. By then, Paboo was living in the shack with Crebe.

And if he had asked her outright whether Petronella was his, would he have been prepared for that responsibility? He never found out, because Mavis left for America.

★

Now, she was still cursing the pastor and encouraging the little crowd to sue the church for all it had.

"Mas Everett, tell the pastor how this affecting your business," she said. "Tell him how it go affect the chicken parts and the cow's milk, how it all a-go spoil."

Paboo knew the farmer was the only one with a generator in the lane. Hurricane after hurricane had set him straight. He had come only to observe the spectacle, standing mute and not giving in to Mavis's hysteria.

Would this send her back over the edge to the insanity into which she'd fallen when she returned from America, shortly after Pearl had passed, and found that no house had been built with the money she'd been sending all the sixteen years she'd been away?

He'd wondered why she hadn't sent for her supposed sister, Petronella, to stay with her in America, why she had decided not to return there after Pearl's death, but he let these wonderings fall away from his mind as the years passed. At first, he'd been happy over her misfortunes, though surprised that he still cared enough to revel in her downfall – until he saw just how deep her distress was.

It began with talking to herself, her hair matting around rollers she wore for weeks on end, and walking up and down the lane, still in her nightgown. People sometimes found her at the fire station hosing her naked body and drying her clothes on the hedges in full view of the firemen, who always took their time before calling Petronella and some-times the police to haul her away. Petronella would bring her some shoes and a windbreaker to cover-up the near transparent night dress.

They called her Mad Mavis in those months. Some claimed that it was all in pretence so she and Petronella could get a place in the poor house and receive other handouts after the landlord threatened to pitch them out of the house Mavis had grown up in.

One time, Paboo had witnessed Mavis walking with Petronella and seem to come to herself for a moment.

"House? We don't own anything here. You think it was easy over there, Pet? I work until my fingers were raw – and for what? I work any job I could get because I find myself in another man country who don't want the likes of me with my black skin in him big office-them, even though I type faster than most anyone I know and have a good head for figures." She took the girl's face in her hands. "Oh Pet, Pet, Pet. My Pet. We worse off than the lady that have to shed her skin at night time. We worse off than even she."

"What you saying, Mavis?" Petronella had turned and looked at Paboo before hurrying Mavis away.

He knew well the story told to him as a boy of the woman who shed her skin at night and how she became a river maid because she had made a sorrowful trade. She had so wanted a daughter that she asked the obeah woman to turn her yam into a little girl, but the woman's life was hard, and she found feeding the daughter a daily struggle so she cursed the daughter for being born. The girl was so distressed that she turned herself back into the yam, and when the woman saw this, in bitterness she ate the yam. At night she found her skin peeling away to reveal scales. When she returned to the obeah woman for a cure, the woman told her that she had traded her desires for a curse and, to this day, anyone who goes by the river at night can hear her wailing in the wind.

Paboo could not see Mavis putting Pet through the pretence of madness, just for the goods and cards and appliances that appeared on her doorstep from the church groups and neighbours who knew and had loved her mother, Pearl. No. It would have been too much to bear. He saw Pet's school mates taunting, laughing, if not at the lean-to school shoes and faded gingham uniform, then at her having to walk the village with her crazed sister-mother.

One day he had called after the pair, running to catch up with them.

"Mavis, I know things is hard right now. You welcome to come and find me or Crebe in the church grounds if you need any assistance." It felt good that he had offered her help, though she had abandoned him in his youth.

Mavis had looked back at him and he became self-conscious about his scruffy beard, bony frame, and faded clothes. Recognition glinted in the deep pools of her dilated pupils. Then, she laughed. It was an ugly sound that he could not forget.

"Why now? You ready to be a father?" Mavis had laughed. "Yes, Pet. Look at him. This is your puppa! This the one that responsible for you being on earth. But ask him what he do. Do he lift one finger to help you all these years?"

"You never said… but you never said anything."

Mavis opened her mouth wide and laughed.

Paboo looked from her to a horrified Petronella, sighed and turned away.

After the church people nursed her back to health, she made it plain she did not need anyone, much less him. When she managed to scratch together a few thousand dollars, she did not return the kindnesses of the women, but pretended that her Mad Mavis period had never happened.

Now, he was looking at the throbbing vein in her forehead as she continued to scream at the pastor.

"Mind your pressure, Mavis," Paboo said, stepping between them. "We can't do nothing until morning. You know the power company don't deal with such things in the middle of the night. What's the use hackling up yourself over things we can't do nothing about?"

"You stay outta this," Mavis said, "You and your good-for-nothing friend don't have nothing to lose, so you can't understand why decent people like me is upset."

"What you do with your life that make you better than we?" Crebe said. "Why you always believe you was better than the people in this here lane?"

A ripple of "uh-hmms" and "Tell-her-dehs" went through the small gathering.

"And I couldn't be scum of the earth if you was once willing to lay up with me," Paboo said quietly.

"Some of you in this community content to be in one state all your life. That was not for me and if I'd had a little good fortune, things would have been different. As for you, Henry Boudan, you talking about lying down with me just because you glad for any association with me. I suppose that was the highlight of your whole miserable life. Right?"

He did not reply. Perhaps she had been reduced to this cantankerous, unlikable spirit because of his failings. But then he could also say that he had enjoyed his life and had lived it as he wanted, without treading on anyone to achieve it.

Then, Petronella pressed through to the front of the gathering. Paboo saw the young Mavis in her face and the sure way she carried herself, even with a squirming toddler in her arms.

"Mama, what you doing down here?" she said.

"Pet, go back up the hill," Mavis said. "I dealing with this. Pastor putting we all in darkness."

It was not lost on Paboo that Pet had never sought him out, not before she left for community college in Manchester, or when she returned to the village with child and husband. He did not imagine that Petronella had been surprised. The story had, after all, been rumbling through the community for years and years. Now he stood two feet from the grandchild he would not get to know because of his own spinelessness.

"But Mama, what you talking about? We have light on our side."

"Light come back up there?" the pastor asked.

"We never lost power," Pet said. "Just those down here."

"I tell you to go back up the hill," Mavis said, walking towards Petronella.

"Mama, you need to stop this. You need to stop this and come home right now," Pet said.

Mavis continued to advance towards her daughter.

Paboo only saw the tail-end of the live wire as Mavis stepped in the puddle. He reached out to stop her, but when a sickening cry came out of her, he knew it was too late.

★

The procession had begun to file out of the church. Straight Finger and Crebe were making their way back to the shack with the shovels and the pickaxe. He looked at the pallbearers carrying out the coffin and remembered the sick feeling that had pooled in his chest when he watched her convulsing body grow still. Petronella had screamed and her child had wailed.

"Well, she gone somewhere else now," someone murmured.

He knew even if he'd had saved her, she would not have been grateful, but still her death gave him no pleasure.

Perhaps he could only have understood her if he had dreamed bigger for himself. He watched them lower her coffin in the ground, noting that more people had been there the night of the blackout than had come to see her buried.

He watched Petronella's little boy take a handful of earth and throw it in after the coffin. It reminded him of himself at eight, doing the same for his own dead mother.

He looked up to see an owl perched on a branch above him. Had it been there all along? It was a curious bird with its protruding yellowing eyeballs and dirty brown feathers.

She would become a patoo, Crebe had said. Paboo wasn't sure about that, but he followed the bird with some fascination, watching it twitching on the branch with the remnants of an insect in its beak.

If anyone else had seen it, they would have stoned it as an omen of further deaths, but he found the bird calming. He pictured Mavis as a nocturnal bird on her perch, set to hoot at others, just out of reach and never in sight in daylight.

He took one last look at Petronella, her boy, her husband, the minister, and the six others who had gathered to sing a mournful rendition of *Amazing Grace,* then he followed Crebe and Straight Finger back into the shack until it was time to cover the grave.

BIRDIE

Birdie pushed into the empty church, letting the wooden doors bang against the concrete walls. She spotted the careful way his red and white robe was draped over the throne-like chair on the pulpit, and she knew she had to set it ablaze. She would make the whole damn place burn from steeple to ground. She would make them all remember how they had stripped her of everything – her grandmother, her home, her son.

She ran up the aisle and took the canister of the oil from under the pulpit, where she had seen it many times, oil used to anoint the saved and to light the lamps at midnight vigils. She poured it over herself, and over the reverend's robe, making a small pool around her feet and the ornate chair. There would be no more singing. No more laying on of hands. No more clapping and twirling and getting in spirit. Not in this place. Not after what he had let happen here. There were no tears now, but she was shaking with something else entirely.

She looked up into the choir loft and saw the hymnals neatly piled on the piano. She tossed the empty canister at them and watched the books topple to the ground, but this did not satisfy her. She began ripping the music sheets from the books down to the spine, grunting with every motion. All those years ago, they had said she could not sing in the festival, she could not represent the church with her big belly for a man they all knew but no one would say aloud.

The tears came hiccupping, ugly and deep from her diaphragm. She felt the oil trickle from her thick curls, down her back and through the folds of her cotton dress. Wiping her eyes, she looked for the box of matches that was just in reach next to where the canister had been. She snatched them up. Then she paused.

Could she leave Jacob? Could she really leave her son?

Just now, he had refused to come to her, had made as if he did not know her. She had defied her banishment, had come back to this godforsaken, back-o-wall Bramblewood to take back her child. She had stood outside the church, away from view under the guango tree and watched the women with tied heads and the men in bush jackets file out after service to shake the hand of Reverend Eugene Hawthorne, his red and white robe regal under the glare of the afternoon sun. Her pulse had raced and the bones began to twitch at her temples. Then, she saw the little boy. Her little boy.

He was chewing the begonia stalks near the steps of the church and she knew him immediately. His face mirrored hers, and he was doing something she had done herself countless times when she was a girl, when her grandmother was still inside the church dancing and chanting with the warner women and could not see her sucking the tender green stalks of the plant.

She stood transfixed, watching him, wondering how she could have let herself be persuaded to give him up. Then she saw the reverend's wife, Rachel, take his hand and the little boy squealed when she tried to take the plant from him.

Birdie had walked out from under the tree unsure what she would say, but something about the gentle way Rachel held him grated on her. But when she had revealed herself, had ignored Rachel's surprised enquiries and had called to the boy, he had clutched the folds of Rachel's floral skirt and pressed himself away from Birdie. She had tried to smile as she knelt and opened her arms, but Jacob had burrowed deeper in the folds and whimpered. It made her ache.

When Jacob turned one, Birdie had been walking across the stage at graduation at a new high school on the north coast. She could not forget that her child was being cradled by another woman, or learning to walk towards the man who had abandoned her. In the earliest days, she would hide crying in the bathroom when her breasts were still swollen with milk, the pain tearing at her insides. When he was two, she had been working for a woman in Montego Bay as a shop-front girl, but every little boy entering the shop was Jacob, even the ones entering primary school in khaki pants and gingham shirts.

Then, just as she had settled into the drudgery of work, a letter came in perfect cursive, but without an address saying: "You grandmother got strokes. She in the bosom of the Lord."

One month late.

She knew then she had to return to Bramblewood to take back her child before he too was lost to her.

Birdie had not been there to say a word at the funeral, but she had cried for her grandmother because she was the only one who truly seemed to love her. She had cried even though her grandmother had been the one to bring her in front of the reverend, had shown him her uniform taut with their shame and said she believed what her granddaughter had told her and that she knew all the police constables, and corporals and inspectors for miles, and they would have no trouble putting a man of God behind bars. She had cried for her grandmother even though the woman had told her the story over and over how it was River Mumma that had come for Birdie the night she was born, but had taken her mother instead.

She cried for her grandmother though she had told the reverend he should take the child.

But her child had rejected her. Like her mother, she was damned. She had come into the world as Hurricane Gilbert was ripping a path of destruction through the island, so she would not go out quietly.

She wiped the tears that had mixed with the oil on her face. Her fingers trembled as she opened the box and took out a match. She looked up to see the reverend in the doorway, peering up at her quizzically. His face was hard lines and shadow, so different from when he was just Eugene and she was his Birdie.

He was coming toward her now in the pulpit. Without a word, she struck the match.

REUNION

Michel Badeau looked down at his son smearing jagged strokes of red crayon across a crudely drawn face, but he didn't really see him. He was thinking about Marisol, how certain he was he'd seen her walking across the road to Dillard's earlier that day.

He'd still been grasping the dry-cleaned shirts his wife had asked him to pick up when he ran after her, the plastic bags flapping and his chest constricting with excitement. He had bellowed at the woman, planted hands on her shoulders and spun her around – to find an unfamiliar face.

Perhaps he'd been thinking about her so much lately, his mind had conjured her right there in the street.

He glanced at his cellphone, then back toward the kitchen where Carmen was slicing chicken for Tuesday paella.

He was sick of Tuesday paella.

It had been ten years since he'd made love to Marisol in Boscobel, Jamaica, but two weeks since he'd run into her at the Atlanta conference.

Their last moments together came back to him full force when she appeared in a red dress at the top of the stairs in the conference hall. He must have looked a fool standing there, slack-jawed, watching her descend.

"Stranger," she said, with a quick, brisk hug. "You don't change one bit, eh?"

She still loved vibrant colour and that light citrus scent.

"Ah... Bonswa! Kijan ou ye?" Michel said. "Must be the cold up in Michigan preserving me."

"Hey! I saw your name on the panel just now, but I wasn't sure. You stayed in Michigan to teach?"

He told her he'd stayed after he got his doctorate and was in Atlanta just for his presentation, where all of ten people had come to his panel on the representation of black men in contemporary fiction.

She laughed and he wondered if she caught how his eyes studied the curve of the mouth he'd kissed a hundred times and how her hair still curled big and wild around her face. A whopping twelve people had come to hear her talk about the Jamaican folklorist, Louise Bennett Coverley, she'd said with a laugh.

As they walked to the exit, he didn't miss the ring on her left hand.

"He's from Ohio. His name is Tom Hendricks," she told him later over two shots of tequila in the dimly lit bar. "Yes. He's white."

He showed her a photo of himself, Carmen and Daniel, their five-year-old.

"You look very happy," she said, handing it back.

He nodded. How could he say it had taken him three years to recover from losing her, after her sudden disappearance during graduate school? It had left a searing in his flesh that had healed unevenly.

They had met over Edith Wharton in a Women's Studies class, he the only male, they the only brown faces. Marisol had come from Kingston to Michigan City, first to study classical piano, then literature, then folklore instead. They bonded over their Caribbeaness and their distaste for the cold. He began teaching her Haitian Creole, she, Jamaican Patois.

In those two years together, Marisol had consumed him

whole. He remembered her breasts soft yet firm in his mouth, like just-ripe mangoes and just as sweet. He remembered their playful sparring about authors and her habit of leaving him lines of novels as obscure riddles all over his apartment.

"Does Carmen write too?"

"She's an accountant," he said, ordering them Scotch.

"How was Korea?" he asked.

"Foreign," she said with a short laugh, "In Seoul, at least, I didn't feel as conspicuous as in the more remote areas. I never got used to being stared at and my hair fondled like I was a sheep in a petting zoo."

"C'mon, Mari! That bad?" he said, using her pet name before he could stop himself.

When she had left him, he promised himself to steel his heart against her and here he was downing Scotch with her, revelling in her every word.

"I liked the kimchi and teaching," she said.

They were quiet for a moment. He looked at her ring and thought how this diamond was four times the size of the one he had given her before she suddenly announced she must go to Korea to teach English.

"I just need a break from this suffocating programme!" she had said to him that day, throwing herself back into his bed as he was making it, spreadeagling her naked form there and looking up at him, still holding a corner of the comforter.

"I win a fellowship and they don't even acknowledge it on the department's page, but let some white male drivel fall into a publication and they talk about it at meetings, in emails, on flyers, in your damn mail box!"

"They aren't always in our orbit!" Michel had offered.

"And that's just the problem with you. You think *everything* is coincidence."

"And you talk like the black Americans. Not everyone is out to get us!"

"You need to open your eyes. You are a black man in America, wherever the hell you from. You think that – "

"How do you know what I think if you *never* ask me, if you keep *telling* me instead?"

She wanted to know why he always sought their validation, like he wanted to be their "good Negro".

He remembered the anger that pressed across his temples as they argued. Of course he had felt his difference. A woman had called the campus police as he sat in the park out in the snow one night. He almost went to jail for wanting solace, but being labelled instead as suspicious. He saw the way many white women tensed when he walked by them on the streets. It was exhausting to consider whether he should feel insulted or pleased when a professor wrote pages of praise on his essay, as though her low expectations had been thwarted. He felt it would destroy him to indulge these grievances. He could not belabour them as Marisol did. So, they had argued until he succumbed, and she became supple and compliant and they were rumpling the sheets again.

He agreed they would go to her family home in Jamaica to spend the last few days of summer while her parents took a cruise around the Mediterranean.

And then, at the end of summer, she was gone.

"You had enough?" Marisol was saying now, pointing to his glass.

Michel did not look at the glass. His eyes rested instead on her face until she became very still, all the unsaid things thick between them.

"Yes," he said shortly, breaking his gaze, getting off the bar stool slowly, and reaching for his wallet.

"You're still angry," she said as he tossed two bills on the counter.

"About what?"

"I can see that vein, Michel."

He shook his head, slipping his hands into the pocket of his slacks, regarding her with a strained smile.

"This is how it was meant to be," he said.

She gave him a grim little smile, getting up from the stool.

"You could have come with me," she said.

"In the middle of writing my dissertation? You knew I'd lose my funding." The familiar warm pulsing spread across his temples.

He watched her fiddle with her purse.

"Why did you say 'Yes' if you knew you had no intention of marrying me?"

He had said it; the words that had plagued him for years fell heavy out of his mouth.

"You know what? You should have my new number," she said suddenly.

Michel had looked at the card she extended as though it were a foreign object, then turned and walked to the doorway when he felt her arm loop through his, stopping him.

"I'm sorry," she said, squeezing his forearm. "I know I hurt you. I was just... scared... and..."

"Scared of what?"

He looked away, unable to hide the old pain, but hearing her sound so contrite he thought how easy it would be to lean down and touch his lips to hers.

"I don't know. I was selfish then... and..." she said.

"...and impulsive...," he said, continuing to walk.

She stumbled against him as they walked.

"...and still a lightweight." He chuckled despite himself.

Then, he put an arm around her to steady her. He felt her fingers thread his and he knew he was lost.

They came to the street. His hotel was only one block away. They could easily walk there. He would not have time to savour removing her dress. He would press her against the door the moment they entered the room. They would fumble with buckles and zippers. She would open herself to him. His body would become lost in her warmth and her scent.

It would be like coming home.

His pocket buzzed and he stopped, knowing before he looked that it was Carmen. He could feel Marisol's gaze, perhaps willing him to not answer but he could not look back at her as he released her fingers and reached into his pocket for the phone.

"Hi my dear," he said. "Oh yes… It went fine."

He looked back at Marisol who was fumbling with her bag again, not meeting his eyes and Michel felt the cavern begin to yawn and widen between them again.

"Yes… Daddy loves you… Yes, I'll be home soon…"

When he slipped the phone back in his pocket, Marisol was wearing large sunglasses.

"I'm… staying this way," she said, pointing behind her.

Michel nodded slowly.

"Well, it was good to see you," he said, reaching down to hug her, lingering there. "And congratulations."

"Let me know about any book signings," she said, slowly easing out of his embrace.

She had already turned to cross the busy intersection.

He would not allow himself to watch as she crossed.

★

He could not explain what he felt now, sitting in his favourite arm chair, inhaling the spicy aroma of Carmen's

Spanish dish. That morning he had broken into a sprint, his pulse racing with the thought of seeing Marisol again. Why he was trying to reclaim a thing long dead?

He got up from the armchair and walked to the doorway of the kitchen where Carmen was leaning over the pot.

"It will be ready in a moment. Go away! Sal de aquí!" she said, smiling over the pot, not looking at him, her curly black hair in a sloppy bun the way he liked.

Michel went up behind her, locked his arms around her waist, and kissed her neck.

"I love you," he whispered in her ear.

"I know. I know. Now go away. Let me cook," she said, patting a hand over his and using the other to stir the pot.

Michel turned her around and kissed her forehead.

"I *really* do," he said.

He felt her go still against him.

"Is everything okay?"

"Everything is fine," he said, running a finger down her jawline. His smile was met with her furrowing brow.

"Daddy, look!" Daniel appeared at the doorway with his completed drawing.

"Ah… bravo!" Michel said, examining it.

He went across to the fridge, and placed the drawing beside a gold-starred school test, Carmen's grocery list written entirely in Spanish and her note reminding him about the dry cleaning.

He touched the note, the sick feeling of loss pooling fresh through him.

When he looked over at Carmen, she was back to stirring the pot.

Sighing, he reached into the cabinet for the white dishes they always used for their Tuesday paella.

PRODIGAL

Angela stands there for a while, suitcase in hand, looking at the overgrown, familiar garden. The bougainvillea vines creeping up the rusted railings, weaving together red, white, and purple blossoms, both mesmerize and paralyse her. The yellow crotons and old man's beard are still there, hiding patches of discoloured and chipped paint. Years in Atlanta have not made her lose her love of this haphazard garden, and she wonders how she could ever have left this little house in Falmouth, Trelawny.

Picking up the suitcase, Angela walks up the stone path. The house is still. Her family is never usually this quiet, but then this is no joyous reunion.

Can she still call them her family?

She stops when she spots the old red pick-up van parked in the garage. It is the worse for wear, but it comforts her that it survived the tumult of her marriage.

She walks up the cobbled stone steps that Kwame had lain by hand and taps on the door. When no response comes, she turns the knob, but it doesn't budge. So, she hikes up her flowing summer dress and steps over the overgrown grass to the backyard. She half expects to see Kwame feverishly thrusting the fork into the earth as she has seen him do a hundred times, and half dreads, half anticipates their encounter after so long.

There is no one there, so she calls again, then pushes the door. It swings open.

"Hello?" Her sandals click through the silent house.

She looks around at her mother's touches everywhere – from the colourful hooks with the hanging pots in the kitchen to the makeshift nurseries of mint plants growing in old juice cartons on the window ledge.

But what has changed since she left?

The dining room seems a little bigger with its newly painted salmon walls and sparse, handmade, rose-wood furniture. The adjoining living room is unchanged, still with the cream settees she had bought in a Christmas sale seven years ago, just before she left. The coffee table is new, unvarnished cedar wood. She runs her fingers across the surface.

Kwame's work.

Angela jumps. Someone has come into the room. The girl's braids are rumpled and hang to her waist. Angela cannot believe that this slender teenager looking at her now, eye-to-eye, is little Della. Now, she has a defined waist, hips and a bosom. Angela smiles and begins to walk toward her.

"Angela," Della says evenly, taking a step back. This stops Angela's advance.

"Della…" Her voice trails off, not sure how to engage. That Della has called her by her first name and not by any term of motherly endearment feels like a jab, but it is not surprising.

They last talked three years ago on her birthday. Della had said little, and Angela had not known what to say beyond the obligatory greetings.

"You know Grandma's funeral is Saturday, not Friday, right? Daddy sent out the wrong information," Della says evenly now.

"Yes… I know," Angela answers. "He called…"

Della is already retreating. Angela realizes she has been

wringing her hands together like a school girl. She pulls out the chair at the dining table and sits down. She presses fingers to her temples and tries to regain her composure as Della slips away into her room and closes the door. Angela undoes the bun at the top of her head and lets her curls loose. They frame her face.

Kwame's voice on the phone had been just as detached as Della's had been: Her mother was dead. It was sudden. He was sorry. The funeral was Saturday. That was all.

He did not call her "Annie" as he had done for ten years. He did not embellish as she tried to make sense of his words. Eventually she'd replied: Yes. She was still there. Yes. She would take the next flight out. Yes. She would pay for everything. No. She was not bringing Paul. There had been no Paul for years. Could she stay at the house?

She is not sure what she had expected of either of them, but it has left her feeling hollow. The worst is realizing that her mother's kidneys had failed while she was trying to live like a woman with no past in another country, with a man who had abandoned her in the same way she had left her own family.

When Angela was growing up, Olivine was rarely sick. When she left, her mother was still dancing dinky mini during festival time. In fact, Miss Vee, as she was known throughout the community, had a stamina that promised she would outlive them all.

Angela does not realize she is crying until she has to wipe her eyes. She finds Timothy looking at her curiously. She straightens in surprise. He, too, is now so tall, now all elbows and knees.

"Mommy?" he says, his face open, his hands full of guavas.

It is the way he says it that makes the tears spring again.

It is as if he is that seven-year-old again, seeing her after one of her business trips. She expects indifference as Della has shown, but he dumps the bag of guavas on the table and she feels his two skinny arms gruffly holding her.

"You're so big! You're so big!" She alternates between pushing him away to look at him and squeezing him close.

"Go and get the bags out front before someone takes them." Kwame's voice filters into the mix of crying and laughing.

"Yes, Daddy," Timothy says, rushing out.

"I can't believe he's fourteen," she says, forgetting herself.

She looks at Kwame's unsmiling face and sobers, wiping her eyes again. He has come through the living room holding two bags of Styrofoam cups and some ice.

"Wasn't expecting you until tonight," he says.

"No… I got an earlier flight. I thought I told you. You need me to do anything?"

"No. No. I had plenty help," he says.

They regard each other for a few stiff seconds. She isn't sure if he is exhibiting anger or indifference. *Could he still be angry?* She used to be able to tell the difference. He looks the same – same tall frame, same dark brow, same brown eyes, same firm jaw line – except he no longer has a potbelly. She wonders if that means he has stopped drinking.

"We having the wake here?" she asks, just to say something. Where else would they have it?

"Yes," he says, walking into the kitchen. "We can expect the whole lane."

Angela has hoped for at least one night's rest before she sees any of the neighbours.

"Of course. Of course," she says following him. "Everybody loved Mama."

She is back to not knowing what to do with her hands.

Timothy pulls in the large suitcase, stops and looks in his father's direction.

"You will be in Vee's room. That alright with you?"

"I don't mind," she replies.

Timothy lugs it away.

"Sorry, one of the wheels broke," she calls after him. She turns to find Kwame looking at her, and she wonders if he can tell she has gained twenty-five pounds since he last saw her that fateful afternoon a lifetime ago when she had cherished her thin figure.

With each year away, the weight crept on. She imagines it must be a stark change for Kwame to see, especially as she is almost a foot shorter than he is. She tucks a hair out of her face nervously.

"How long you staying?" he asks.

"A week. I'm not sure. I don't have to rush back."

The truth is she is not sure she can re-enter the United States as her work permit has just expired, just when she decided to leave for the funeral, and her contract at the public relations firm has not been renewed. At the airport, on her way out, they told her she had overstayed by six days and detained her for three hours.

"You seen Della? She's around here somewhere. She's in her room all the time now," he says, putting the bags of ice in the fridge.

"Yes," Angela says. "I saw her."

She wishes he would not be so polite. He must have more questions. Angela cannot believe how casual he is, how easy he seems. On the phone, he had seemed guarded, cold even. It had been long enough, but still she had half-expected an outburst. He has simply resigned himself to live without me, she thinks bitterly.

"She's taking it hard," he says, turning on the tap, his back to her. "Vee was like her real mother."

He stops and looks over his shoulder at her.

Angela turns away. She cannot dispute it.

In the beginning, she had tried to stay involved. She would talk to her mother and her children every week. She knew that even if she and Kwame could not make it together, that even though she had run off with a local entertainer to another country, she was still a mother. Then the weekly call became every fortnight, then every six weeks, until they were only for holidays and birthdays – and that too fell away. She had missed all the milestones. Della had become a woman without her, but even if Kwame said aloud what she knew, it still smarted to hear it.

"I never mean to make you feel bad, Angela," he says turning to her, sighing, "but, she and Vee was close, even when Vee have to punish her for running off her mouth. She was there for her. Jus' the reality."

"I know. I know," Angela says, around the lump in her throat. "I am grateful to Mama."

She hugs herself. Kwame turns back to the sink. Angela turns to leave the room.

"Oh!" Kwame says, turning around. "I forgot to tell you that Rachel lives here now."

"I see," is all she says.

She should have known with all those tacky doilies and black pigmy figurines all over the living room furniture.

★

It has given Kwame some measure of satisfaction to tell Angela this, but he has actually become very fond of the woman Angela had sent to draft papers for their divorce. Rachel was so unlike Angela – warm, uncomplicated, eager to please.

No. He was not going to apologize that he took some small pleasure that this had gotten under Angela's skin. Rachel had not found his career a disappointment. He was not a mere carpenter; he was an artisan. Angela had begged him to find a *real* job, one where he would wear a shirt and tie and blend in seamlessly at her music clients' events.

He goes outside now and tosses the last of the coal bits into the old coal pot, then piles some dry sticks and some dry grass to kindle the flame. He lights it, stoops to blow on the embers, and thinks about the people who will come to wish Vee well.

No one has ever said it to his face, but he knows that the men called him soft and the women foolish. They had watched him with his young children going to the church harvest, or into town for new school uniforms, to Della's festival competitions, to Timothy's school shows, conspicuously without Angela. He had continued his life with an outward show of indifference that had served him well.

Yet, every night, alone in his work shed, while the children slept, he drank himself into a stupor. Angela had not liked when he drank, so he drank all the more until Della found him lying face down and had wailed because she had thought he was dead. Vee told him that he had best find a new way to ease his anger, or she would be taking the children away from him and clear across the island.

He fills the tall, cylindrical soup pot with some water and sets it on the hearth and begins peeling the yams and sweet potatoes. He grew these himself alongside Vee's kitchen garden. He and the old woman had not gotten along for much of the time he and Angela were married, but the shared abandonment had sparked a kinship between them.

One evening, he had come in to find Della printing sums in an exercise book, and Vee beside her, squinting through old spectacles at the pages. It was hard to believe this was the girl he had threatened to lock in her room if she did not do her assignment. The old woman had looked up at him, and he'd returned her reassuring smile.

When Vee got sick and started the rounds of dialysis, he had sat in the pick-up trying to compose himself at the thought of losing her.

He had still been in a haze after Angela had blindsided him, so he had been the last to realize that Rachel was inventing ways to see him, asking to verify this document or having to redraft that document – much to Vee's displeasure.

After Angela had been gone for six months, Vee had said, "You don't see that woman always around here fishing around you. Calling here all the time. You blind?"

He had laughed, thinking that his mother-in-law despised anyone that was not her daughter. It was only after he had broken his ankle and Rachel had driven an hour from Havendale to Old Harbour Bay and had made him gungo peas soup, when Vee had gone to a night meeting, that he finally began to see.

In the beginning, he would still speak about Angela when he was with her, and it pained them both, but Rachel had a way of touching him that calmed him, her consoling hand rubbing away tensions from his shoulders, his knuckles, his chest, his abdomen. She brought with her a soothing calm that even Della began to respond with less searing looks, and Timmy became less wary of the new woman coming with them on the summer trips to St. Thomas.

As Kwame peels the corn, Della comes out of her room. She stands in the doorway, still wearing the pink dress she has been in for the past two days.

"You want some help?"

He looks back at her. She looks so small, so meagre. The

dark circles under her eyes make her appear skeletal. He is happy that she has resurfaced. He worries when she sleeps all day like this. He had gone by her room the night before, wanting to talk to her about Angela's impending return, wanting to hear her concerns. She had ignored the wreath someone had left on their doorstep, not bothering to open the door, not bothering to take it inside. He feels that in some way he has abandoned her too, leaving her alone in her grief.

"Okay," he says, holding out the corn to her.

They stand side by side at the sink, pulling off the husks, in silence for a while.

"Why is she staying here?" Della asks.

Kwame pauses for a moment.

"Because she is your mother, and her mother just died."

"Is she going to be moving back in here?"

"No," Kwame says. "I don't believe she will stay."

"Good," Della says, and Kwame feels her lean her head against his shoulder. He puts his arm around her and squeezes her briefly.

"Now, hurry up," he says, squeezing her one last time. "People will soon start coming. Mas Reid coming with the other musicians to set up and I need to go pick some breadfruit."

★

Della continues to pull off husks, then break the cobs in two. It helps to be doing something, as though the action can unknot the tangle of feelings in her chest.

When she was younger she was always a little afraid of her father. Perhaps it was the tension she'd witnessed between her parents. He always seemed in a perpetual state of anger and annoyance.

He changed after he met Rachel.

She recalls how she could hear, even when she and

Timothy were in the house, the way her mother would shout. It didn't stop when their grandmother came to live with them, though Granny Vee had brought them solace, even as she, Della, was trying not to think about how her family was falling apart.

"You have to have a calm spirit with the earth to plant good things," Granny used to tell them in the garden. "The earth will return to you what you give it."

Timothy comes into the kitchen now.

"You know you should at least try to talk to her," he says. "You can give her a chance."

Della does not respond.

"You only have one mother," he continues.

Della throws the corn in the sink and turns to face him.

"She stopped being my mother when she left."

"You can say anything. People change." He opens the fridge and takes out a Red Stripe beer.

"You mad?" Della takes it from him and puts it back.

Timothy opens the fridge and takes it out again. "Look like you think you are my mother?"

"Fine," Della says, turning back to the sink, scooping up the husks and tossing them in the trash. "Do what you want."

She goes back in her room and opens her window, careful not to break the intruding limb of the cherry tree. It is not much of a view. All she can see is the huge Julie mango tree in the neighbour's yard, and a cow wandering near their fence about to ravish her father's young ackee tree. She makes no move to shoo away the animal.

She remembers when she won the spelling bee and came running up those back steps. She had watched her grandmother take off her gloves and twist the medal around and around in her hands, smiling. She still remembers the hug, how her bosom smelled of primroses and earth.

"Quick, go show yuh mother," Olivine had said, almost pushing Della toward the door, but she did not need much coaxing.

"Well, who stopping you?"

Della had stopped in the kitchen as the sounds of angry voices filtered in from the living room.

"Cannot take no more of dis!"

It was her mother's high-pitched shriek. "I have to do this for me, Kwame. For. Me. Just this once! But you would not understand that."

"What about the children, Angela? They don't matter? What about them, eh?" Her father's voice had boomed.

Della had placed the medal on the table and crept to her room. What was happening? America? She'd been lying on her bed, sniffling and staring blankly at the ceiling when the door clicked open, and her mother held up the medal asking her what it was for. That was the last time she had let her mother see her cry.

★

Timothy watches from the steps as people come in. The band is on its third cycle of "Tell Me If You Ready Fi Go". He takes a sip of the beer and stashes the bottle among the ferns near the steps. He watches his father handing out cups of hot mannish water. He watches Rachel giving cups of white rum to some men leaning against the fence. He sees Angela standing on the other side of the backyard watching Rachel hand out the cups.

He has grown to like Rachel, but has always hoped his mother would come home. He wonders how he can make his parents rebuild the family, especially now that Granny Vee is gone.

He looks at Miss Atkins, their neighbour, come in the yard dancing all the way, tossing up her white skirt, throwing back her white scarfed head. He scoffs, remembering that this is the same woman who called the building inspector on Granny Vee, to have them cut down the ackee tree she claimed was leaning over the fence into her yard. Now, here she was singing along: "Tell me if you ready fi go… Uh-huh… Tell me if you ready me fi go… Mm-hmm… Are you ready to go…"

He does not understand the purpose of a nine-night other than giving people an excuse to go to a dead yard and stuff themselves at the expense of someone else's grief. He hates the din, the excess, the chatter. He takes another sip of the beer. He does not like the taste, but likes the way it lulls him. They will be here all night, but he has already told his granny goodbye. He pours some in the bush to wish her safe travels, then puts the bottle to his head.

She was always firm with him. She would not approve of his drinking the beer, but she would not have told his father either. She would have cuffed him upside the head and told him, instead, another version of the cautionary story of his grandfather, the Guinness, and the motorcycle crash.

He looks at his mother now. Miss Atkins is hugging her, but he does not believe it is full of the feeling the woman's animated face implies. Angela is saying thank you to them, looking lost, standing there swaying awkwardly to the staccato sounds of the keyboard, the brash bass pulsating and the man endlessly singing the same song.

He thinks about the letter he wrote his mother when he turned nine, begging her to come back and the disappointment that came when she said she could not, not just yet. Yet, he could not hold onto the sorrowful, angry feeling as long as Della has. He watches her serve fried fish and bammy on plastic plates. She does not look as sallow as she did earlier.

"Tell me if you ready fi go… Uh-huh…"

Timothy gets up and goes inside. The beer has begun to make his head swim.

★

Angela knows her mother would not have liked this fuss, the people coming in and trampling on her garden, gyrating to this music, but she knows it is the expected way. It does give her a good feeling seeing the throng, knowing how loved Vee was.

She looks again at Rachel with her perfectly flat-ironed hair and thin physique. She does not remember her being this pretty or this smiley, but it's Kwame she watches now. He seems altered. She remembers how he would avoid having to deal with any of the industry people she brought home, having to pander to them, but here he is playing host effortlessly. She watches him lean over and say something to Rachel and notes the tender way she holds his shoulder.

At times, when Angela has woken up in a foreign place thousands of miles away, she has wished she had never left, but could never see a clear path back.

She can still hear her mother's voice telling her that a parent must put her child above herself.

"I am doing this for them, Mama," she had said on the day she decided to leave. "It's not right for them to see us fighting all the time, and plus, this opportunity in America is going to give us much more stability."

"If you think is the right thing to do," her mother said, in that way that always irritated her. It was full of disapproval, the go-and-see-for-yourself challenge, but said in a warm, round tone. Angela didn't reveal that another man had turned her head, the kind of man she had always envisioned for herself – a man without calluses and broken English or silences she could not understand.

If she had still been a girl, Vee would have told her a tale, like the time she was eight, had disobeyed and picked the starapples meant for market before they were ready. When she suffered a painful stomach ache, her mother said it was punishment enough, but she told her the story about the boy and the drum and how his mother and father warned the boy not to go into the bushland to hunt for food that day.

"Why not?"

"Because it was dangerous," Vee had said. "Because children need to listen to the wise counsel of their parents. Sometimes we see trouble long before it comes."

"Did he die in the bush, Mama?" she'd asked.

"No, dear heart," Vee said. "He did not die. The rains came down, and the boy came across a tortoise who gave him shelter in a little house, but the tortoise meant him no good and when the boy was drying himself in one of the rooms, the tortoise stuck him in a hollow drum and covered him with the skin of another animal. This skin he got from an obeah woman who put a charm on it, so the boy could not come out on his own. He stayed in there three days wishing he had listened to the warning and only when the tortoise beat the drum and the boy was made to sing did his parents hear his voice from afar off."

"And then he died, Mama?"

"He could have, but his parents loved him so much they found a way to free him, but not before he learned his lesson. They tricked the tortoise with the promise of a grand dinner."

"With oxtail or peppered steak and fat crayfish?"

"Yes. I suppose he liked those things as much as you. The tortoise ate and ate, and while he was eating, the mother went and cut the special skin off the drum and released her child, and before the tortoise could reach him, the father tossed him into a waiting pot of boiling water. The boy listened to his parents after that."

"But they killed the tortoise, Mama. Is a sad story," she had said with a laugh.

"Yes. They did it to save their child. Now go wash your hands and come and get this soup."

"Is it tortoise soup?" She'd broken out into giggles but did as she was told.

Now, Angela sips the mannish water and lets its warmth spread through her. She also lets herself weep silently.

Am I too late, Mama?

She looks up at the darkened sky, and the stars wink at her through her tears. "Mama, if you can hear me," she whispers, "I miss you. I'm so sorry."

She presses her fingers to her lips and holds it up to the sky. She wonders if she has lost the only person who loved her completely. She looks over at Della walking toward her. The girl quickly extends a plate of fish and bammy to her.

"I'm a vegetarian," Angela begins to say, "but it's okay. It's fine."

She grasps the plate. Della lingers, seeming to hesitate.

"Did you make any of it?" Angela asks.

"Yes. Granny Vee taught me how to soak and fry the bammy and how to fry the fish, so it is crispy but not burnt." Angela looks down at her hands where she is holding one side of the plate and Della is holding the other.

"Then I would like to try it," she says.

Della shrugs, releases the plate, and walks away. Angela watches her daughter walk away from her for the second time that day.

Perhaps all she can hope for is to atone. In time.

She looks over at the singer-man who has finally begun to play a new song, and Angela begins to sway again.

CECILE

"Hey, String bean! You don't see is the wrong uniform you wearing?"

Cecile was sitting under the tamarind tree in the school yard during the mid-morning break when Ezra, a stocky boy in her grade six class, found her.

Soon, a group of laughing children congregated as Ezra continued, "String bean! String bean!"

He didn't stop his singsong chant until he drew the tears that had been just below the surface at assembly. Then, Cecile had suffered the stares as the only one in green and gingham in a sea of brown and beige. Her grandmother had said it would be another two weeks before she got her new uniform.

Making fun of her for wearing her old school's uniform was one thing, calling her "String Bean" was quite another; and then when the girls from her class played sightings with an old juice carton ball at break, they didn't ask her to play.

"Laugh wid dem, Ce-Ce," her granny advised, "What you think I do when they call me 'Queenie' because my mother used to starch even my bloomers?"

Cecile said she did not really care what these children at that fool-fool country school said, because her mother would soon come back for her.

Granny May sighed heavily and handed her another piece of jackfruit.

Cecile had not wanted to leave Kingston for Granny May's three-room house that sat on an acre of farm land.

Her mother, Elouise, had told her the news quite casually one morning.

"You going to your granny house for a while, Ce-Ce," she said, grating a little extra nutmeg into her bowl of hominy porridge. "Is not for long. I going to stay with your Auntie Mitsy in Miami."

The next day, her mother put a whimpering Cecile, still in her all-age school uniform, on a bus to Manchester, and with a kiss and a wave, was gone.

It was a week or so before Cecile found out that her mother had turned herself into the police on fraud charges, hours after sending her away.

★

After her first few days in Christiana, Cecile sought out refuges from people like Ezra, such as the dwarf almond tree under which she now sat, near the very edge of school grounds.

As she sat watching a woman hang sheets on her clothesline, Cecile heard a crinkling sound. She turned to find a girl opening a piece of foil and biting into a sandwich. The girl stopped chewing when she caught Cecile staring.

"Is what?" she asked, glowering.

The girl was at least half a foot shorter, and this made Cecile smile.

"I'm in Grade six – B," Cecile said. "What grade you in?"

"Grade six – C," the girl answered grudgingly.

"So why you eating all the way out here?" Cecile pressed.

"I always come out here." The girl continued to eat. "You notice me never ask you why you wearing a different uniform and why *you* in *my* spot? By the way, is true that you whole family get kill off in a turf war?"

"What?" Cecile stood up and faced her. "You country pickney don't know nothing about me. My mother in Miami if you must know."

Cecile noticed the girl was looking over her shoulder and followed her gaze to a boy in a torn merino and fraying shorts pulling a cart laden with plump crocus bags along the trainline.

"Shane!" the girl said, racing over to him.

The boy left the cart and walked to meet her at the fence. The girl nodded at something he said, and he patted her shoulder. Cecile noted that this smiling girl was the one who had tried to appear menacing moments before.

They looked back at Cecile and laughed. The smile forming on Cecile's face quickly dissolved.

Then, the bell rang.

"Who is that?" Cecile asked, as the girl ran by her.

"My brother Shane."

"What him say?" she asked, running after her.

"That you ask too much blinking questions."

★

"I should get my right uniform next week," Cecile said hesitantly when she found the girl sitting on the stone near the barbed wire fence a week later.

She was wearing a white shirt and a brown skirt, which Granny May felt was as close as she could find to the uniform.

"*You* back again?" the girl asked. "You hear from your mother in foreign yet?"

Cecile used a stick to draw in the earth. She looked back and frowned at the girl's smirk.

She had heard from her mother, but purely by accident.

One day, after school, Cecile had found an envelope Granny May left on the old piano with her mother's name on it. It did not have an airmail stamp like those her father or her Aunt Mitsy sent, but came from a place called Fort Augusta.

Cecile snatched it and went into the backyard. The looping words said that Elouise was sorry to burden her mother with Cecile, that she did not know how she would manage to survive the next four years in prison.

She lingered over the words: "Don't bring Cecile for visits."

She folded the letter, put it back on the piano, crawled under the outside steps, and wept.

"Yes," she said very forcefully, as if the lie had to be dislodged from her throat. "She going to send for me to go to Miami too."

"At least your mother far away," the girl said. "I wish mine was too."

"You don't mean that."

"You can say anything. You don't know that woman."

"Is it because she don't make your brother come to school?" Cecile asked.

The girl got up and looked over at the train line. "She have to choose one, not both," she said solemnly.

Cecile looked at her but didn't know how to respond.

"I going to get a suck-suck from the tuck shop," she said finally. "You coming?"

But as she said that, Cecile spotted Shane climb over the fence and walk toward them.

The girl's face lit up. Cecile saw that he was as ragged as he was the first time she had seen him.

"Why you girls don't play ring game like normal pickney?"

"You act like you too big, when you turn eleven next month just like me," the girl said.

"You're twins?" Cecile asked.

"Twins?" Shane laughed.

"Him have a different mother," the girl said quickly.

"Tanella, stop tell story," Shane said.

"Was just a little joke, man," she said, chuckling.

"We grow up in the same community," Shane said.

Cecile looked back at Tanella who, with folded arms and pouting lips, was feigning outrage.

"No wonder they call you 'Pit Mouth'. You tell too much lie, man." Shane laughed.

With one motion, Tanella reached up and slapped his head. "You really use that name that Ezra call me?"

"You won't like it if I hit you back," he grumbled.

"Ezra always calling people names," Cecile said.

"See. String Bean understand."

"Don't call me that."

"What? String bean? String Bean!" Tanella turned and stared full into Cecile's face.

Cecile did not remember hitting her, but suddenly Shane was pulling them from the dust where she was pummelling Tanella with tight fists.

"Tanny! Why you mus' trouble people so?" he said as they struggled in his grip.

When her breathing settled, Cecile looked over at Tanella, whose braids were coming loose and sticking up around the crown of her head. Her socks and face were brown with the savannah dust.

Tanella broke out laughing and pointed at Cecile whose white shirt now had streaks of cow dung and was ripped right down the front.

Cecile looked down, screamed, tugged off the shirt, and crossed hands over her bare chest.

"Is what you hiding?" Tanella asked. "You no even have no breast yet."

The bell rang, but the three of them just stood there.

"I live over that train line," Tanella said finally. "I can lend you a blouse."

"I not going anywhere with you," Cecile said, dropping her hands at her side.

"Well, go back, and let the principal deal wid you," Tanella said.

Cecile decided that going to Tanella's was better than having to explain her nakedness.

"Is that house there," Shane said, pointing to one of the dilapidated wooden houses with the bamboo stalks and the clothes line. Cecile stared at Tanella who was no longer smirking.

"I never can understand you girls," Shane said, as they walked towards the fence. "If anybody should get one lick up him head-side is that boy, Ezra."

Tanella laughed. "No. The only way to catch that little piglet is through him gut."

"One time, this girl at my old school did pour pee into a teacher's passion fruit drink," Cecile said.

"Piss? Yes, we should do that!" Tanella almost fell over the fence in another bout of giggles. "Can you imagine him face when he see what him really drinking?"

★

Tanella's yard was strewn with rusting tires and the hull of a car. Bottle fragments littered the red earth. Tanella made no acknowledgement or apology. Shane had left them at the barbed wire fence and had pushed the handcart in the opposite direction toward town.

The house was just as decrepit inside. Cecile knew that her grandmother had little but always managed to keep a clean house. When she had lived with her mother in Kingston, they had far more, and they had a helper who came once a week to keep it in order. Now, looking at the scandal bags strewn all about, the trail of red dirt, the heaps of mouldy clothing, the piles of yam skins and orange peels, Cecile wondered if she wanted to borrow Tanella's blouse.

"Come! Come!" Tanella called as they went into a room.

Cecile stopped short when she saw a woman lying on a floral sofa that sagged halfway to the floor.

Tanella turned around to look at Cecile.

"Is okay. She not dead," she said casually, pointing to the bottle on the floor. "She just finish her morning rum."

"Who is she?" Cecile whispered, following Tanella into the next room.

"The woman that say she is my mother." Tanella closed the door behind them.

As Tanella riffled through a drawer set, Cecile looked around at the unpainted walls, the bare mattress, the dingy sheet hanging as a makeshift curtain at the window, Then, Tanella was holding out a faded T-shirt to Cecile.

"Is my P.E. shirt. You can borrow it until tomorrow."

Cecile sniffed it. It smelled faintly of cake soap and moth balls.

"Why you smell it so?" Tanella looked hurt. "You not even say thanks."

"Sorry. Thanks," Cecile said, quickly pulling it over her bare skin.

A roach crawled out from under the bed, and Cecile jumped. It swooped into the air and perched on the hanging sheet.

"You never see cockroach before? Even city girls know about roach."

Tanella went to the window and looked out. Cecile followed, sitting on the ledge beside her.

"I staying here until my real mother come for me."

They could see the school pavilion from where they sat. Cecile wondered how many licks she could get for missing the bell, or if she could get suspended for something like this.

"You don't think she is your mother?" Cecile asked.

"No. Them tell me they find me out at the Church of God as a baby, and this lady decide to take me."

Cecile looked at her warily. She watched Tanella bend down and pick up a dog-eared grade-six reader.

"Is like this one," Tanella said, turning the pages, "The mother used to brush her daughter hair at night, hair that long long down her back, like river maid. This girl stupid and give pure talking to. If I have a mother like that, I wouldn't so fool-fool. I tell that lady out there that one day me ago run 'way and find my real mother."

Cecile remembered the time when her mother told her she could not get the grater cake Granny May had sent because she had failed Language Arts. Cecile had gone to her room, closed her eyes tightly, and prayed her wicked mother gone – the mother who brushed *her* hair for school, who had even let her press it out with the hot comb and had curled the bangs when she was the flower girl for her Auntie Mitsy's wedding.

Cecile wondered if she should tell Tanella this story.

"You think my real mother could have hair like that, long long down into her back?" Tanella asked in a small voice.

Cecile saw that Tanella's eyes had become glassy.

"Maybe," Cecile said. "A girl with coolie hair in my class used to have to plait up her hair and wear it in a high bun it was so long."

Tanella chuckled and wiped her nose. "That hair you can buy out at Miss Daphne shop," she said.

They sat like that for a moment, looking at the drawings, not saying anything.

Then, they heard stirrings in the next room. Tanella dropped the book and moved the sheet. She deftly removed two of the wooden louvres and squeezed through the opening in the window.

"Come on. Her hand heavy when she ready."

Cecile followed suit, climbing through. They ran across the backyard all the way to the barbed wire by the playing field.

When Cecile got to the fence, she lingered halfway over it, and looked back to see a figure in the window. Her heart sank to see the woman's drooping, bloodshot eyes.

She thought of her own mother sitting in a cell so far away from her and wondered if she now looked this haggard, this distressed. Perhaps she would write her a letter to say that she had begun to forgive her, to say that this country school was not so bad, that she had found a friend, but she wanted her back and loved her still.

"Hurry!" Tanella shouted, already near the dwarf almond tree.

Cecile jumped down. She would ask Granny May for money for postage stamps. She followed Tanella, sprinting clear across the field.

ABOUT THE AUTHOR

Wandeka Gayle is a Jamaican writer, visual artist, and Assistant Professor of Creative Writing at Spelman College. She has been awarded writing fellowships from Kimbilio Fiction, Callaloo, the Hurston/Wright Foundation, and the Martha's Vineyard Institute of Creative Writing. Gayle has a PhD in English/Creative Writing from the University of Louisiana at Lafayette. Her writing has appeared or is forthcoming in *The Rumpus*, *Transition*, *Interviewing the Caribbean* and other journals.